YO-DWP-224

THE ZOOKEEPER'S MENAGERIE

By Joanne Duncalf

Twelve Star Press

The Zookeeper's Menagerie
Copyright © 2008 by Joanne Duncalf
Published by Twelve Star Press

For more information, please contact:
duncalfj@goldfieldaccess.net
joanneduncalf@yahoo.com

Book design by:
Arbor Books, Inc.
19 Spear Road, Suite 301
Ramsey, NJ 07446
www.arborbooks.com

Printed in the United States of America

The Zookeeper's Menagerie
Joanne Duncalf

1. Title 2. Author 3. Fiction/Politcal Satire

LCCN: 2007904387

ISBN 10: 0-9797232-1-3
ISBN 13: 978-0-9797232-1-6

Dedication

I would like to express my deepest appreciation to my mother for introducing me to the wonderful world of allegorical fantasy through reading. Also, I wish to thank my family and friends for their patience and encouragement during this quest to fulfill my dream of penning a modern day rendition of my favorite childhood fairytale, *The Wizard of Oz*. And, most of all, I would like to thank God for the inspiration He has blessed me with.

Long live the Zookeeper,

Joanne Duncalf
November 2007

CHAPTER ONE

"Mariel, wait up!"

Mariel glanced over her shoulder and saw a living Barbie running toward her down the school hallway. The curly haired blonde girl was garishly dressed in a red-and-white-striped blouse and dark-blue miniskirt, and her white boots were immaculate. Painted silver stars sparkled on her cheeks, matching the twinkling silver fringe on her boots.

Mariel groaned inwardly and slammed her locker shut. "Beth, what are you doing here? You should be getting ready for the parade with the others."

"Oh, I have time, Mars," answered Beth carelessly, tossing her blonde curls. "It's summer and they aren't strict about punctuality on this parade, anyways. I just came back to keep you out of trouble. You look great by the way." Beth swept a cursory glance over Mariel's form-fitting navy jacket and matching knee-length skirt, embellished with a white carnation and a tiny American flag pin at the lapel. With her almost-black hair swept up in an elegant French roll, Mariel looked like she'd stepped out of a JCPenney catalogue.

Mariel looked askance at her best friend, shifting her books to the opposite arm. "You're referring to the Rules, I presume." Beth stiffened, and Mariel nodded ruefully. "I thought as much."

Beth implored Mariel with her large green eyes. "You *are* going to change your address, aren't you?"

Mariel lifted her chin and started down the student-congested hallway, her heels clicking on the black-and-white-checkered linoleum. "No, I'm not. I'm class valedictorian and I worked hard for that honor. I will deliver the speech exactly as I wrote it."

"But Principal Higgins said—!" cried Beth in horror, hurrying after her.

Mariel flashed a smile over her shoulder. "It's Independence Day, Beth. I intend to celebrate freedom. *My* freedom."

"Oh, but I still think it's a terrible—"

"Beth, please. I've made up my mind."

"Mars, will you come to your senses!" Beth practically wailed, coming alongside her friend and gesturing with rigid hands held out pleadingly toward the resolute girl. "You wouldn't get away with half of this madness if you weren't so

2

popular…though I still think it was dreadful of you to turn down Josh Greeley."

Mariel cocked her head. "What about Josh Greeley?"

Beth's cheeks colored a telltale shade of pink. "What about Josh Greeley?" she repeated, incredulous. "Any girl in this school would give her right arm for one date with him, and he asked you to go steady!"

Mariel narrowed suspicious blue eyes, glancing up and down the florescent-lit corridor before lowering her voice. "Does everyone know about this?"

Beth didn't bother lowering hers. "It *is* true, isn't it?"

Annoyed with how fast gossip could travel through a small-town high school, Mariel nodded reluctantly. "It's true. He did ask me."

"And you said no?"

Mariel nodded again.

"Oh, how *could* you?"

Mariel pretended to consider that. "I don't know. What was I thinking?" She snapped her delicate fingers. "That's right. I was about to say yes, but then I suddenly remembered that the last girl Josh dated was Tammy, and she wound up pregnant."

"Yes, but he'll be more careful next time! I heard him say so. He'll use…*protection*."

Mariel chuckled dryly, twisting sideways in mid-stride to squeeze past a knot of laughing students absorbed in discussing plans for the rest of their summer vacations. They were taking up the whole corridor. "Do you even know what the failure rates for condoms are, Beth?"

Several heads turned their way, but neither girl paid attention. Beth was almost beside herself. "Who cares? It's *Josh Greeley!*"

"And I have both my arms intact," returned Mariel coolly.

3

"But not your head!" Beth squealed, beyond exasperated. "Do you have any idea what dating Josh Greeley would do for your popularity?"

"I have an inkling of what he would try to do to my honor."

Beth rolled her eyes and seized her companion by the shoulders, spinning Mariel around to face her. "Look, Mars, I don't know what's with you. We've been best friends since first grade and I understand you less and less all the time! *Josh Greeley* asked you out and you had the nerve to refuse? He's the hottest boy in this whole school—maybe in this whole town!" Mariel shifted uneasily as if to free herself from Beth's grasp, but Beth held on tighter and wouldn't release her. "Get a *clue*, Mars! You act like it's such a big deal to sleep with somebody, but you know what's a big deal? While you're still spouting your non-sense about honor and condom-failure rates, other girls are dating the hot guys like Josh Greeley and you're *missing out*! You're gonna be left with some nerd like Butch Brown!"

Mariel blinked, stunned into paralysis by Beth's outburst. The two girls stood staring at each other. Coherence was slow to return to Mariel's numb mind, but when it did, it brought with it the realization that they were standing at the center of atten-tion. Slowly, she looked to one side, then the other, meeting pair after pair of familiar eyes—most of them girls, teenagers who existed in Mariel's vast and varied clique. The red-headed freckle-faced Fay Hart, the Latino cheerleader Annabel King, and tall, lanky Nannie Farmington stood out among the others. Only they weren't looking at Mariel with the usual admiration they'd shown in the past for the popular valedictorian. Now their stares consisted of mingled disgust and contempt.

Mariel's mouth went dry. For once, the girl who always knew what to say was at a complete loss for words. The noisy hall had fallen dead-silent.

"B-but Butch Brown is…is gay," Mariel stammered in a voice that wasn't quite her own.

"Precisely!" Beth nearly screeched. "Everyone thinks you are, too!" The rising tide of murmurs that broke out drowned Beth, but she increased her volume to make herself heard over the affirming masses. "Maybe by the time Butch Brown gets his act together, you will, too!"

"Or maybe you won't," put in Nannie Farmington, folding her skinny arms and looking down her long nose at Mariel.

Indignation choked Mariel. Besides the unsavory direction these accusations were taking, she felt like she'd been thrown into the Coliseum by her friends and now stood at the mercy of the lions. How did this happen?

Bewildered, Mariel drew a difficult breath. "I'm not gay."

"Then go out with Josh Greeley!"

"But I'm not interested in him," Mariel retorted uneasily.

"Then who *are* you interested in?" chimed in the red-headed Fay Hart.

"I've never heard you talk about *any* boys you wanted to date since our freshman year," Beth pointed out.

Mariel's mouth dropped open. The ring of students was closing in on her from all sides.

"Yeah. Maybe there's something *wrong* with you," murmured Annabel King.

Blinking rapidly, Mariel backed up against the lockers and found herself with no place else to go. She shook her head. "It's not that I—" she tried to explain.

Suddenly, a deep voice boomed over the loudspeaker. The head of every student jolted reflexively heavenwards.

"Attention students! The parade will begin in five minutes. Please report to your designated areas immediately."

The tension in the hall snapped like a rubber band. There was a mad scurry of feet, and a rush of activity away from

5

Mariel freed her from the hammer and anvil she'd been caught between. Abruptly, Mariel found she could breathe again. Teenagers were drifting by her, and she felt like a forgotten island in the sea of people—which was temporarily relieving. Then Mariel turned and saw Beth hanging back, glowering at her with a half-pout formed on her full lips, before the blonde left her best friend and ran after the crowd.

In the empty hallway, there was only the faint buzz of the florescent lighting and the stale scent of lemon detergent to occupy Mariel's senses. She closed her eyes and leaned against the cold metal lockers. The same student body that once held her in high esteem had become her enemy in a matter of minutes, and she was still recovering from the shock. Luckily, she didn't have to be at her designated area for a few more minutes…

Because when those few minutes were up, she was going to have to face a second den of lions.

CHAPTER TWO

Green Valley High School presented the best in small-town entertainment, so it was no wonder the entire population of Green Valley turned out at the school every year for the Fourth of July festivities. Locals decked out in red, white and blue flocked to the football field, filing in on the heels of the grand parade—which consisted of a mounted mule rider, the entire Green Valley High School contingent of six cheerleaders, a fat brown llama, a scruffy fellow dressed as a patch-eyed pirate with a green parrot on each brawny shoulder, a handful of misfit mutts and a scrawny orange kitten. There were also two huge tractors; one red and one green. Each tractor pulled a colorfully decorated hay wagon that carried Green Valley alumni who were celebrating their class reunions. They were sitting on bales of hay, waving enthusiastically at their friends and family. Leading the procession was a festively balloon-clad fire truck with flashing lights and a couple of firemen perched on the back, waving nonchalantly at the bystanders. Once the parade made the circuit of the entire town, it drove into the parking lot outside the football field. The fire truck was the only thing that did not march inside.

Mariel watched this ceremony from atop one of the high open-air bleachers, where she sat alone with her elbows on her knees and her chin propped in both hands. The six baton-twirling cheerleaders—Beth among them—were first to take the field, and they started to perform a simple choreographed routine that excited the onlookers into a flurry of applause.

Everyone acted like it was such a novel show, when this exact same program was repeated without the slightest variation year after year. Right away, Mariel noted the absence of Roy Farmington, Nannie Farmington's father, but that could only mean his arthritis was acting up again. Mrs. Shoemaker was herding eight unruly children—six boys in stained trousers and two girls in rumpled dresses—to their seats while bouncing a pouting baby on one large hip and gripping one of her young boys—whom Mariel remembered as Bobby—by the back of the collar. It was a vain attempt to keep Bobby from shooting rubber bands at the prim old maid, Peggy Apricot, who sat stiffly in an old-fashioned lavender dress, working her knitting needles at a furious pace and staring formidably down her spectacled nose at those who crossed her path. The long-standing Green Valley joke was that if the president ever created the Department of Gossip, Peggy Apricot would be nominated to be its Secretary. She was certainly qualified.

Donald Barker, the plump mayor who liked to wear a bowler hat and a fancy gold watch hung from his traditional waistcoat, strode importantly towards the low stage, where he would shortly—and very predictably—give a long-winded monologue touting the greatness of Green Valley and the magnificence of its inhabitants, the "little people."

To prove his latter point, the school valedictorian would be called upon to deliver a speech. This year, that meant Mariel Stone.

"Mariel! Ahoy there, lassie!"

Mariel swiveled her head, already smiling at Kurt Miller, who was impersonating a pirate this year. Again. He always chose a pirate costume, which was most likely due to the fact that he owned two parrots and never missed an opportunity to show them off.

"How's the eye patch wearing?" Mariel called back.

Kurt seated himself in the row one section to Mariel's left and grinned, feeding his parrots saltine crackers. "The world has lost its third dimension, lassie," he replied in his contrived pirate accent. "Can't hardly see a bloomin' thing."

Mariel laughed. "Well, at least it looks good."

"Why thank ye, lassie, that's the main point. Where're yer parents at?"

"Sailing the seven seas," said Mariel grandly, "but by air. They're on a trip to Europe."

"Oh, was that this week?"

"Yes."

"Argh, I forgot." Kurt flicked cracker crumbs from his purposely unshaven cheek, which gave him a pirate's roguish look. The twin parrots munched eagerly at their treats, sending more showers of crumbs down Kurt's dirty cream-colored tunic.

"That's all right. My parents would have forgotten, too, if I wasn't around to remind them. Now I'm home alone." She clapped her hands to her cheeks in an imitation of the popular movie.

"Orphan for the week, aye?"

"Orphan forever, if they discover the delights of European chocolate."

They shared a chuckle. The remainder of their conversation was interrupted by a burst of applause at one of Annabel King's athletic tumbling routines. Laughter followed when one of the pink pigs, dressed in more frilly lace than a doll, broke loose and chased a gray scamp of a dog across the opposite sideline. Grunting fiercely, she tottered after the whimpering mutt who hopped away with a bewildered expression in his homely eyes. A gangly teenage boy in dirty overalls came running behind them, holding his straw hat with one hand and trying to step on the pig's loose leash with a kangaroo-like foot.

A gruff throat-clearing behind the bleachers caught Mariel's attention. Turning from the fascinating spectacle of Green Valley in all its glory, the girl was discomfited to find Principal Higgins glaring up at her.

"Miss Stone, you have the correctly edited copy of your address, I presume?"

Mariel fidgeted. "Um-hm. Er, yes, sir." It was the truth.

"Good. I expect you to abide by all the Rules. You *do* remember them, don't you?"

Mariel nodded without meeting his eyes. "Yes, sir." That was also the truth.

"Very well." Principal Higgins was always worked up about something, and some of the students wondered if continuously high levels of stress contributed to his flushed cheeks. He scratched them whenever he was agitated—as he was doing now. "Then I'll expect you to omit the name of a certain *deity* whose very existence is questioned by some of this country's most esteemed minds, Miss Stone."

Mariel lowered her eyes and dared not answer. Higgins was implying that her beliefs stemmed from a simpleton's lack of worldly knowledge. She bit back her multitude of arguments.

At that moment, there was a shrill whine and a collective gasp from the audience. Mariel whirled in time to see one of the rockets, which was supposed to be set off in the evening hours after the potluck supper, streaking prematurely into the sunny skies with a blaze of orange sparks. The explosion went off like a gunshot, and red sparkles fell like glitter that snuffed out before making landfall.

All eyes turned towards the stand of remaining fireworks to visually determine the cause of the mishap, and a guilty little boy's head poked out. It was another one of the Shoemaker children—one whose name Mariel couldn't recall. Mrs. Shoemaker was already on the field, lumbering like a giant gumdrop towards the miscreant. Mariel shot a glance at the remaining Shoemaker clan. Temporarily free of supervision, all of them developed a severe case of the wiggles, two involved themselves in a shoving match over possession of a toy Corvette, and Bobby was aiming rubber bands at Peggy Apricot again. Seconds later, an offended yelp from the old woman confirmed a direct hit.

By the time the pyromaniac youngster was collected by his harried mother, Principal Higgins was gone. Mariel looked around and found him stalking towards the fireworks stand to have a word with Mrs. Shoemaker, and Mariel breathed a sigh of relief that she was spared further questioning. She couldn't wait to get this ordeal over with.

But it was not to be.

"'Tis bad luck," growled Kurt the masquerading pirate from a few seats away. Mariel became aware of an eerie tension which had settled over the gathering, and she rolled her eyes at their superstitious nature. The fireworks show was always choreographed with special care, and the rockets were almost sacred.

Peggy Apricot's hyper knitting needles were remarkably still. "N-nothing of this magnitude has gone wrong at this celebration in fourteen years," stammered the resident historian and acknowledged source of all information pertaining to Green Valley. Pressing her spectacles against the bridge of her nose, the old maid prophesied gravely in her crackling voice, "It'll come to ill, mark my words! The last time we had an accident on the Fourth of July, McGuffey's tool shop burned down the very next week."

"Puh-KAW! Puh-KAW!" hollered one of the pirate's shoulder parrots indignantly, turning his back on the football field with a flap of his wings and lowering his head to sulk. A few people exchanged worried glances. The green bird's response confirmed Peggy Apricot's prediction of doom. No one noticed one of Bobby's rubber bands slip out of the parrot's feathers and fall between the stands to the grass below.

The impatience of Donald Barker triumphed. Disregarding the activity continuing around the fireworks and the murmurs in the audience, the proud mayor took his rightful place before the podium and began his well-rehearsed speech, gesturing dramatically like a circus ringmaster throughout its entirety. Principal Higgins shot him an annoyed glance and reluctantly stumped off the field. Mrs. Shoemaker trailed in his wake, bouncing the baby on her hip and gripping the back of her son's shirt. The disturbance caused by her return to the bleachers and the subsequent restoration of law and order among the rowdy children blotted out a goodly portion of Donald

Barker's sermon on the virtues of Green Valley. The Corvette-deprived boy sent up a progressively louder wail. Those unfortunate enough to find themselves sitting behind the Shoemaker clan craned right and left with irritated expressions, hoping to see around them.

Suddenly, Mariel felt a sharp sting in her shoulder, and she cried out, nearly losing her balance. Her hand, thrown out in the nick of time, barely saved her from a nasty tumble off the bleachers. When she pushed herself upright, she found Bobby snickering and aiming another rubber band at her. With a swift gasp, Mariel ducked and watched the rubber band sail past her ear. She sat up again with a warning look at Bobby, and she heard a voice calling her name.

"And now, testament to the grand achievements of the Little People, I give you this year's Green Valley High School valedictorian, Mariel Stone!"

Mariel shot to her feet, rattled. The moment had come sooner than she'd anticipated. Amid a smattering of applause, Mariel clumsily descended the rows of bleachers, trying to smile and pretending not to notice the rubber band that bounced off her jacket sleeve. Mayor Donald Barker stepped down and met her halfway. He shook Mariel's hand, and she gave him a stiff nod in return. She walked the remaining distance across the field with a show of more outward calm than she felt and mounted the platform, setting her two pages—with the unabridged copy on top—on the podium. Then she raised her head and waited for the polite clapping to subside, willing the knots in her stomach to magically disappear.

A quick scan across the sea of faces revealed mixed emotions. Many of those who were formerly part of Mariel's faithful following now stared darkly back at her. Principal Higgins was watching her like a vulture. Beth sat in the front row with her similarly dressed cheerleading companions, their batons and pompons limp in their laps. Peggy Apricot's knitting needles were humming again, and the old lady's sharp gaze bored into Mariel. Kurt Miller was busy with his parrots. The baby gurgled and sucked his fist as Mrs. Shoemaker bounced him on her knee, and Bobby was actively searching for another target.

Only Donald Barker beamed at her with pride. Mariel Stone was the latest great product of *his* town, and this was her chance to shine. Mariel flushed and couldn't help returning the mayor's smile. She looked down at her page, cleared her throat, and began.

"The fact that I, Mariel Stone, am the valedictorian at Green Valley High School is a privilege and an honor. Throughout most of history, educating women was not a common practice. Women were not given rights equal to those of their male counterparts. Women had to fight for the freedom we take for granted today."

Every woman in the audience sat up straighter. The feminist slant in the opening paragraph appealed mightily to them. Even Peggy Apricot looked almost pleased.

"Christopher Columbus had to battle to convince influential people that his theory on the spherical shape of the world was correct. Once our ancestors braved the wild seas and settled in this land we now call America, we had to fight for our independence from England."

Those two sentences set Mrs. Shoemaker to yawning and her children into fits of wiggles. History was not a subject that held them captive.

Mariel glanced up at them, then nervously plunged on, determined not to lose them altogether. "This country's character was forged in the fires of warfare," she announced, shaken by their reaction. Mariel steeled herself. "Our Founding Fathers built this country on the principles of freedom—freedom of speech, freedom of education, and freedom of religion." She took a deep breath, missing the sign Principal Higgins waved to the soundman. "The cornerstone of this country is God, and God has—"

Abruptly her microphone went dead, and her voice turned hollow in her own ears.

"…blessed us with…er, with…"

Mariel trailed off uncertainly. She tapped her microphone with a frown, then looked up quizzically—only to meet the malicious glare of Principal Higgins turned fully on her. Understanding washed over Mariel. Hiding her severe disappointment by squaring her shoulders, the girl drew herself up as Principal Higgins began to clap, as if her speech had reached its conclusion.

"Bravo, bravo!" called the principal. "Well-spoken!"

Slowly, the bewildered audience joined in applauding Mariel's address, though they seemed surprised by its shortness.

Mariel forced a smile at the crowd just as the sun was blotted out under a covering of gray, and Mariel slammed her hand down on the podium to prevent her papers from flying away in a sudden gust of wind. She jerked her gaze to the skies and saw a thunderhead, which she hadn't noticed earlier, now moving swiftly over them. There was a great flash of lightning and an ominous rumble of thunder shook the ground. Surprised, people craned their necks to see the atmospheric disturbance for themselves, and Mrs. Shoemaker held her baby close as he wailed in fright.

The mayor made a face, but there was nothing for it. He stood up on the lowest bleacher seat, held up his arms, and made an official announcement. "Today's festivities have been cancelled until further notice. Citizens, get home before the storm hits!"

His words were met by a mad scramble. Metal bleachers banged under the trample of feet. Peggy Apricot looked a little pale as she stuffed her precious knitting supplies into a cloth bag. Kurt Miller was trying to soothe his parrots and maintain his balance as he walked carefully downwards amidst a rush of humanity. Mrs. Shoemaker was herding her children onto the field as the owners of the various parade pets collected their animals while trying to keep them from bolting away in terror. The squealing pigs strained at their leashes and the teenage boy had his hands full trying to hold them. The mule's ears were flat and he was half-bucking, braying wildly. His tense rider managed to climb off the shying beast and tugged on the reins, but the mule fought harder and tossed his head in stiff defiance. Then he sat down on his haunches and refused to budge. The cheerleaders scrambled for their accessories.

Suddenly, Beth gasped, and her eyes widened as she made a terrible discovery. Her hands flew to her face. "Oh, my gosh! I can't find my pompon!" she was wailing. She whirled from side to side, searching frantically. "Where's my other pompon? Has anyone seen my pompon?"

Her pleas were lost in the melee. The sky was getting darker. Discarded bits of trash blew across the ground. When Kurt Miller finally emerged from the hurricane of activity, he looked around the football field. Mariel Stone had vanished.

Far away from the chaos, Mariel ran down the deserted road in her stockings, clutching her high heels and both copies of her Fourth of July speech. She rushed past dilapidated buildings with fading signs and a tumbleweed rolled across her path, but Mariel looked neither right nor left. Her vision was already blurring. Her throat was hot and dry, and she was sick to her stomach, and it was all she could do to keep from breaking down and crying in the middle of the desolate two-lane road.

As the storm closed in, she focused on running. The pounding of her own feet and of her broken heart were the only sounds that filled her ears. Just as she turned the corner and ran into her neighborhood, the skies opened and unleashed a mad fury of pelting rain.

By the time Mariel stumbled into her own house, she was soaked to the skin. She shut the door behind her and leaned against it, rapidly losing the battle with her tears. She padded wearily to her room and peeled off her drenched suit, which she'd picked out so carefully for this special day, and she tossed it aside in a crumpled, forlorn heap. She pulled on a pair of soft sweats and a T-shirt, already sniffling. The raindrops dismally slapping against the windowpane wept with her for the lost respect, and even hatred, of an entire town that once belonged to her. With that thought, Mariel threw herself onto the bed and cried herself into a miserable slumber.

Hours later, Mariel opened her eyes. It was dark, and the rain had stopped. The air was eerily still. A faint sheen of moonlight spilled into the room and painted the wall a delicate shade of silver. With a moan of weary heartache, which came after shedding so many tears, Mariel flipped her pillow and rolled over to face the wall, closing her eyes again.

Abruptly, she stifled a cry and sat bolt upright in horror. The shadow of a man was lurking outside her window!

CHAPTER
THREE

Mariel pressed herself against the cold wall, her heart thudding in her chest as she watched the shadow on the wall. The silhouette came close, then moved slightly to the left and right, as if he were peering through the window. Then he nonchalantly drifted away and disappeared from Mariel's sight.

Mariel didn't dare move. Hyperventilating, she stared at the spidery patterns of tree shadows on the wall, waiting for any sign of the stranger to reappear. Minutes crept by, and there was nothing but evening silence and the occasional fall of a clinging raindrop left over from the day's storm.

Mariel almost allowed herself to give in to cautious relief when suddenly a horrible thought struck her. Living in small-town, relatively crime-free Green Valley, it wasn't a habit of hers to lock the front door. And unless she was sorely mistaken, she hadn't bothered with that minor detail today, either…and that meant an intruder could be in her house at this very moment!

As if her sheets had grown unbearably hot, Mariel sprang from the bed and landed in a crouch on the carpet, her wide eyes sweeping over her room. A weapon! She needed a weapon. Preferably something heavy. Mariel's desperate glance fell on her bedside lamp, and she yanked it, plug and all, from the nightstand and crept towards the door, trailing the cord behind her.

Breathlessly, Mariel peered around the doorframe into the hallway. Nothing moved. Either that meant he hadn't thought to try the door, or…maybe he hadn't made it around the perimeter of her house yet! Maybe there was still time to stop him!

Determined to reach the front door before the unknown stranger did, Mariel gripped her lamp tighter for courage and moved into the hallway, letting her hand brush across the wall so she wouldn't lose her way in the dark. She didn't want to risk turning on the light, and she knew the house layout like the back of her hand.

The living room was just ahead of her, a lighter shade of moonlight blue against the blackness of the tunnel that was the hallway. Everything had grown in the dark, and seemed to be at least twice its normal size. The furniture cast ominous shadows across the floor and Mariel felt the hair on the back of her neck standing on end. The familiar living room had taken on a creepy quality, brought on by fear of who or what might be lurking there. She reached the corner and pressed her back against the wall, then leaned forward slowly to peek around the edge…

Nothing. Her breath caught in a rush of relief. The front door was not far away now, and she could see it dimly outlined as a white rectangle against the evening grayness, and her progress was slowed when she stepped on the lamp cord. She kicked it away irritably and tiptoed to her destination. Her hand closed over the lock, and with a wonderfully satisfying click, the house was secured.

Lowering the lamp, Mariel stepped out of the entryway and gave a muffled scream when one of the shadows rose to life. The shadow shouted and moved away. Mariel herself scrambled backwards in a wild panic until her back hit the front door, and she stood there, staring in terror at the other-worldly apparition. She held out the shaking lamp, and it quivered and rattled in what was supposed to be a threatening manner.

"Stay back! Stay back!" she yelled.

"All right…all right!" returned a male voice, frightening Mariel further. He took another step backwards. "Look, I'm just—AHHH!"

There was a mighty crash as the intruder tripped over the couch arm and fell hard on his back, his booted feet flying into the air. Seizing her opportunity, Mariel dashed forward, leaped over the couch with a sharp battle cry, landed on the carpet and whacked him over the head with the metal base of her lamp.

"OW!"

Mariel hadn't hit him with all her might, because she couldn't will herself to, but it was hard enough to elicit a cry

from the fellow. He threw his arms over his face to shield himself from any future blows and cringed. Mariel inwardly
recoiled at the idea of hitting the man again, and during her
hesitation he rolled onto his stomach and crawled away from
her, backing against an easy chair like a cornered animal.

"Don't hurt me! I mean you no harm!" he insisted.

Mariel held up her lamp, not convinced. Her bold attack
had quelled the worst of her terror. "Then what are you doing
in my living room?"

In the dim moonlight, Mariel saw him eyeing her lamp
warily, his expression tense. "I was just looking for you, Miss
Stone, and I didn't see you at the window so I tried the door
and—"

Mariel blanched at the mention of her own name.
"How...how do you know who I am?"

The poor man took his time answering. He dropped his
forehead into his palm with a low moan, obviously in pain.
"The...the Zookeeper told me."

Mariel gave a snort. "That's ridiculous. We don't have a zoo
in Green Valley."

"No...no...of course not. The Zookeeper isn't from
here...either..." He trailed off again as a wave of pain swept
over him, and he went on with an effort. "It was the announcement at the football field. They called you Mariel Stone."

"Oh. That explains everything." The events of that awful
afternoon returned to Mariel in vivid detail, complete with the
bitter aftertaste. She felt even less inclined to politeness
towards the fellow for reminding her of it. "So it seems I've
made yet another enemy, is that it? That's why you've come
after me?"

"No...no..." He was suffering, but Mariel couldn't tell
how much of his injury was being faked to play on her inherent sympathies. He groaned softly and looked up at her. "I'm

not here to hurt you. I'm just bringing a message. Please, I'll tell you everything, but can I get some ice for this? My headache is killing me."

Mariel fidgeted and weighed her options, and their possible consequences. What a lousy week for her parents to be away! But she couldn't ignore his plight, which she was responsible for, so against her better judgment, Mariel gave in. She stood back and let him stumble his way past her into the kitchen while she clutched her lamp.

Moments later, Mariel leaned casually against a kitchen counter and folded her arms, watching the stranger sit on a chair and nurse a swelling lump on his head, now buried under a plastic bag of ice cubes. The kitchen was fully illuminated, and now that she could see him without any trouble, some of her fear dissipated. He looked normal enough, dressed in a navy-blue trench coat, designer jeans, a cranberry-colored polo shirt and black boots. She judged him to be in his mid-twenties, blond-haired, well-built, and relatively gentle for someone who barged into houses uninvited. But Mariel didn't entirely drop her guard. Her lamp was sitting on the counter within easy reach, just in case.

Mariel's blue eyes narrowed suspiciously. "I've lived in this town for most of my life and I know each and every one of the people here well. Maybe too well. And I've never seen you before. What's your name?"

"Gabe," he answered in a subdued tone.

Mariel lifted her eyebrows. "That's it? Just Gabe?"

He nodded under the icepack.

"What's your last name?"

"I don't have one."

Something about the frank way he said that made Mariel almost want to laugh. She allowed an incredulous grin to cross her face. "What? Why not?"

"Because I don't need one."

Mariel gave in and laughed. "The world is populated by thousands upon thousands of Gabes."

"Yes, but none like me."

Mariel's laughter faltered and gave way to puzzlement. "Of course not, but…never mind. Why did you come for me, Gabe?"

He lifted his bright blue eyes to meet her gaze, though half his face was obscured by the icepack. "The Zookeeper has called for you," he intoned gravely.

Mariel raised her eyebrows. She was not unaffected by the reverence Gabe used every time he named the Zookeeper, but it was infinitely confusing. "And, so, what do I do about it?" she asked, at a complete loss.

"You answer his call. Come with me, Miss Stone. I'll take you to the Zookeeper."

Her first reaction was to blurt out a yes before logic prevailed. Bewildered, Mariel unfolded her arms and stood up straight, staring curiously at the young man. "Wait—wait a minute. Why does he want to see me, Gabe?"

"He has a very important mission for you," Gabe replied, shifting the icepack away from his tender forehead. A nasty reddish knot stood out beneath his blond hair.

Mariel winced when she saw it. She tore her gaze from this fresh evidence of her skill with a bedside lamp and looked into Gabe's blue eyes instead. "Well…that makes no sense at all. If it was so important, why did he choose me?"

"Because of the address you gave, actually." Gabe set the icepack aside and turned his full attention up to Mariel, alternately wringing and clenching his freezing cold hand to bring back stolen warmth. "The Zookeeper has waited a very long time for someone like you to come along. When he heard what you had to say, and saw how you stood up in the face of such opposition, he sent me to find you straightaway."

Excitement tingled through Mariel. The honor of being chosen out of…however many people this Zookeeper had to choose from was heartwarming, and the idea of a special mission being given to her was definitely appealing, especially because he appreciated her much-maligned speech. But Mariel knew better than to pounce on offers that sounded too good to be true, so she reined in her eagerness and tried to think up reasons to decline. "I don't see why he needs me when he already has you, Gabe."

Gabe smiled knowingly at her. "Thank you, but I'm just the messenger. There are many things I can't do." He slowly stood up, keeping his distance, but Mariel was feeling rather fearless around him by then. Perhaps defeating him with a mere lamp had an effect on her confidence, after all.

"Miss Stone, will you come with me and meet the Zookeeper?" Gabe implored her. "He'll explain everything when we get there." Mariel opened her mouth to answer, but Gabe asked as an afterthought, "Do you know how to ride horses?"

"Horses? I…" A shock of realization jolted Mariel's nerves. "Oh, dear, Gabe, you didn't let one in the yard, did you?"

Gabe nodded, smiling again. "Don't worry about North Star, though. He's a very good horse."

"I don't care how good he is, Gabe!" cried Mariel, fairly bolting for the door. "He could cause all sorts of trouble, especially with the neighbors. I don't want to have to explain this to Mom and Dad when they get home!"

Gabe held out his hands, chuckling at her exasperation. "Miss Stone, slow down. He's not going anywhere. Why don't you change into some jeans and meet me outside in a few minutes? I'll stay with him and make sure he doesn't mow down your neighbor's tulip garden in the meantime."

Mariel stopped in the doorway and considered that. "All right. But it's not Emma's tulips I'm worried about; it's her rosebushes. They're her prize possessions and she cares for them like pets." With that, Mariel turned and disappeared down the hallway.

A short time later, Mariel made the acquaintance of the most beautiful white horse she'd ever seen. She could hardly believe her eyes when she saw him standing in the front yard, his large head lowered demurely between Gabe's hands while Gabe murmured affectionate nonsense to the stallion. An ear twitched in Mariel's direction at her approach, and the horse raised his head to watch her. Mariel caught her breath. He was noble and regal as a statue in the moonlight, and he fairly shimmered with silver stardust when he moved. Flames burned in his intelligent dark eyes. Mariel guessed he had Andalusian blood in his background, but his limbs were too fine and delicate for him to be wholly Andalusian.

She took a slow step forward, entranced despite herself. "Is he…?"

"Oh, yes, he's quite tame. Come here." Gabe beckoned her until she was standing before the awe-inspiring creature. "Don't be afraid," Gabe instructed, taking her trembling hand in his and holding it forward. A velveteen muzzle dropped into Mariel's palm and a warm puff of air fell onto her fingers. A thrill of delight went through her at the touch.

"Oh, he's beautiful!" she breathed. Then she looked the huge animal over again. "Are…we going to ride him?" she asked nervously.

Gabe smiled. "Yes."

Mariel swallowed, taking inventory of certain minor details. Among her concerns was the fact that North Star lacked both saddle and bridle. Why was she doing this, anyway?

"He's gentle," Gabe hastened to assure her, seeing the doubt in Mariel's expression. "And see? He didn't behead a single one of your neighbor's precious flowers." With that, Gabe sprang lightly onto North Star's broad back and held down a hand for Mariel. Mariel hesitated, making sure the horse didn't harbor the least objection to a rider before taking it. Gabe expertly whisked her astride, settling her just in front of him. Mariel watched North Star anxiously. He swiveled an ear at her. That was all.

Color rose to her cheeks. "Gabe, I don't think I can do this," she admitted in a small voice. "There's some kind of special mission waiting for me, but already I'm intimidated by a horse. I think I'm going to greatly disappoint your Zookeeper," she told him ruefully.

Gabe chuckled. "There's only one way to find out." He circled an arm around Mariel's waist and clucked softly to North Star. The great horse broke into a gallop and bounded smoothly away, running so lightly over the grass and down the road that he hardly seemed to touch the ground. Her neighborhood was gone before she could blink.

Suddenly, Mariel gasped. The stallion wasn't touching the ground at all! His four hooves glided over the empty air, and the scenery was flying by at an incredible rate. Mariel clutched two fistfuls of thick mane, her eyes wide with fright.

She heard Gabe chuckling behind her. "Relax, Miss Stone. I won't let you fall."

Mariel tentatively released her death-grip on North Star's mane and found there was, indeed, no danger of falling. North Star ran as swiftly as the night wind, but he was as easy to ride as a rocking horse. And Gabe was still holding her tightly. Mariel raised her head and let the wind blow freely through her dark hair.

They raced away into the night with Mariel still wondering why she'd agreed to go on this mad adventure with a stranger she'd met only a short time before. If she'd seen the yellow glitter of unfriendly eyes that watched them pass beyond the Green Valley city limits, she would have changed her mind right then and gone straight home.

CHAPTER FOUR

When Mariel opened her eyes, she felt extraordinarily peaceful—though somewhat disoriented. She smelled Christmas trees. Dawn had broken, turning the sky pink and purple, and sunlight illuminated the world. She didn't remember falling asleep, but Gabe's arms were wrapped around her midsection, North Star was galloping effortlessly beneath her, and her head was resting on Gabe's shoulder, nestled inside the flap of his trench coat. Mariel gave an incoherent mumble and rubbed at her eyes, yawning.

Gabe looked down at her and chuckled. "You slept well," he observed.

Mariel felt as if she'd never slept better in her life, but she kept her remarks more neutral. "North Star didn't hit any speed bumps."

Gabe's warm laughter calmed Mariel, and she emerged from his jacket into the rushing wind. She narrowed her eyes against the invigorating onslaught and ran her fingers through her tangled hair, which the fierce air current immediately tangled up again. Mariel wisely gave up and looked around, noticing her surroundings for the first time.

Everything was the same...and yet different. It took Mariel a moment to realize that the trees were strange to her. Instead of the familiar deciduous varieties of oak and poplar and sycamore scattered in small clumps over the golden July landscape, there were walls of tall, noble pines looking down on her as she flew past on North Star. The spicy scent of firs, combined with the remarkably fresh air, made her want to breathe deeply over and over again, and she couldn't get enough of the delicious aromas that wakened all her senses and made her feel more alive. Reddish pine needles carpeted the path the white horse rushed over, and sunbeams caught in glades of dancing buttercups. Amazed, Mariel turned to survey the left side...

And found herself staring over the jagged edge of a cliff.

Mariel let out a strangled scream and lurched away so violently that North Star's delicate balance was upset. He tossed his head and whinnied, his front hooves glancing off the ground, and he careened sideways. A huge pine tree loomed before them. Mariel shrieked and clapped her hand over her eyes. They were going to crash...

Gabe shouted, and leaned in the opposite direction to right them, swerving the horse away in the nick of time and saving them all from disaster. Mariel felt pine bark roughly scrape her calf through her jeans and she parted her fingers, peeking out with one eye. Gabe's arm tightened around Mariel's shaking body.

"Be careful, Miss Stone!" her companion clipped out.

Mariel was still trembling from the shock, but she slowly lowered her hand from her face. "I'm sorry...I'm really sorry..."

Gabe sighed, then hugged her close and hushed her. "It's all right, Miss Stone. Don't worry about it. But keep quiet," he added tersely, his eyes searching the trees for any sign of movement. He hadn't mentioned it to Mariel, but some of the shadows were alive.

Mariel meekly nodded and said nothing more.

Once her adrenaline rush had subsided, Mariel glanced over the ledge again, more prepared for the sight of a huge gorge opening up below her, draped with blue-green pines over the immense slopes, interrupted here and there by gray boulders and enclosing a foaming white river winding snake-like through the bottom of the canyon. "We're in the mountains," she murmured softly.

Gabe dragged his gaze from the forest and slowly smiled at her observation. "This is your first time, isn't it?"

Rendered quite breathless by the sheer scope of the majestic vista below, Mariel could only nod as her eyes traveled hungrily up one slope and down another, trying to take in everything at once. She'd seen pictures of such places before, but the best of them—even the brilliantly colored postcard quality shots—couldn't capture such grandeur, or the soaring feelings that stirred inside Mariel as she beheld it with her own eyes, while riding atop a flying horse who knew the invisible trail by heart.

"I never tire of it myself." Gabe's voice was low in her ear, and Mariel realized he was as awed by the mountain aura as she was.

And that's when North Star suddenly veered to the left—and stepped over the edge of the cliff.

For a moment, they were hanging weightlessly in midair, and with a rush gravity caught up to them. Mariel barely had time for a muffled gasp before she realized the white stallion was bounding down the mountainside, nimble as a goat; leaping from boulder to boulder, skipping effortlessly around scrubby pines that grew determinedly among the rocky crags. Amazed by the impossible grace of the equine athlete, Mariel forgot her fear. The downward plunge was more exhilarating than any roller coaster she'd ever been on. Behind her, Gabe didn't so much as shift his seat, and as they rapidly descended, his eyes moved up to the ledge they had just abandoned.

A black wolf stood there glaring sullenly down on them. He was joined by two other gray wolves, both equally frustrated by the departing horse and his passengers. One of the grays bared his fangs and snarled.

Ice shot through Mariel's veins. Her head whipped from side to side, attempting to locate the source of the sound, which bounced off the rocks and seemed to come from everywhere at once. "What was that?" she whispered breathlessly.

Gabe looked away from the wolves as North Star rounded a bend and carried them out of sight. "Something you shouldn't have to concern yourself with, Miss Stone," responded her companion casually. "Just…things you hear in the mountains sometimes."

Chilled as she was, Mariel was disinclined to pursue the matter further. The spell of the mountains had closed over her again, and somewhere ahead of them Mariel heard something she'd never heard before: the perpetual rush of a river. It was getting louder.

And then she saw it through the trees, sparkling white between the dark lines of the firs that thinned as the stallion brought them steadily down the steep rock face.

Swiftly, North Star took them level with the water. Mariel couldn't tear her eyes from the white fury beside her, leaping and churning and splashing between its wide banks. As powerful as the river was, North Star was faster. He broke into a gallop on the flat ground and raced by the river quickly enough that the water seemed to be trapped in slow motion, the curls of swelling water frozen in midair. Only the constant noise convinced Mariel's bewildered mind that the river was moving as fast as the great horse.

That loud rush that already filled Mariel's senses completely was steadily increasing to a deafening roar, and the river ahead abruptly dropped off. Mariel gave a shrill cry, which was lost in the jagged crash of the waterfall, before North Star was again leaping downwards so swiftly that the waterfall seemed trapped in time like a stream of frozen icicles.

The white stallion landed firmly on the ground, and the waterfall resumed its previous course and slammed into the rocky bottom. Mariel watched, utterly fascinated by the deadly force of it. North Star made no move to follow the river's journey and stood there, panting. Gabe's keen blue eyes roved among the trees, and he was murmuring something too low to rightly hear, and Mariel leaned her head back until she caught him in the midst of a number chant.

"What are you doing?" she inquired.

Gabe looked down at her, interrupting his mantra long enough to reply, "Counting to a thousand."

"Why?"

Gabe had to smile, and he paused at forty-seven. "Security purposes, Miss Stone. Please, allow me to finish. The Zookeeper awaits us."

Reluctantly, Mariel subsided. She didn't see how counting to a thousand would secure anything, but her desire to meet this mysterious Zookeeper overrode her curiosity about Gabe's strange habits. She sat quietly, lightly stroking North Star's silky neck, until Gabe concluded with a final glance through the blue-green woods and clucked to the stallion. North Star turned aside and, to Mariel's alarm, headed straight for the waterfall.

"I… I can't swim!" she cried, her frightened eyes flitting back to Gabe. "Please don't tell me we're going *in*!"

Gabe might have chuckled, but Mariel's fear was genuine enough that he politely refrained. "We're not, Miss Stone," he answered confidently. "Trust me."

Mariel didn't see how it could be avoided. They drew near enough to feel the ground shake beneath the waterfall's merciless pounding as a cold spray brushed Mariel's face. But as they approached, Mariel noticed a narrow, dark opening behind the thick stream of pouring water, and North Star carried them inside a cave, his hooves clopping against the stones like an ordinary horse's.

Darkness enveloped them completely. The ground was rough and uneven, providing a jolting ride as North Star trotted along in a choppy up-and-down rhythm—a remarkable contrast to the journey's earlier smooth comfort. Mariel twisted around and looked over Gabe's shoulder to see the portal of light shrinking behind them, and the glittering wall of water turned to a sheet of diamond against the gleaming sun. She stared longingly until North Star rounded a corner and the last bit of light vanished altogether. With a shudder, Mariel faced what she knew to be the front.

Gabe's arms tightened around her momentarily. "I've got you, Miss Stone. Trust me."

Trust me. Those words echoed from the invisible walls and resonated in Mariel's mind. It was a lot to ask of her, seeing how Gabe was still practically a stranger and she was venturing into the unknown. What appeared to be absolute black nothingness might have concealed anything. She'd read stories of caves like these containing bottomless abysses that yawned open without warning and swallowed up intruders. In some of the more imaginative tales, explorers fell down…and down forever. At the time, Mariel had easily dismissed that as pure fiction, but now that she couldn't tell the difference between blinking and staring ahead with open eyes, she began to wonder how much truth there really was in those books.

Mariel's other fear was colliding blindly with a wall, and she tried to remember if horses could see in the dark. But judging by the smooth, confident manner in which North Star moved forward, twisting and turning more times than Mariel could guess in the infinite blackness, he either *could* see in the dark—or else he knew the endless passage, or passages, by heart. Mariel might not have trusted Gabe yet, but little by little, she was beginning to trust North Star. The steady ring of hooves on stone surrounded her, and she mentally clung to the small comfort of sound, since her sight was cut off completely. Her other heightened sense was touch. The stallion slid easily beneath her with the grace of a great cat, and Gabe's arms wrapped around her kept her from even the illusion of falling. At least Mariel trusted Gabe more than the oppressive darkness, and she leaned back against him, welcoming the safety of his embrace.

Gabe gave an unseen smile. "We're almost there, Miss Stone."

"You can call me Mariel," she told him, glad for the sound of another voice.

After drifting for what seemed an eternity in formless oblivion, Mariel's sight caught on a tiny pinprick of white light somewhere in the distance, shining like a little star. The star grew until it clearly outlined a sunlit emerald opening, and before Mariel knew it North Star brought them blinking into full daylight.

Squinting against the brightness, Mariel couldn't see much. But even before her sight readjusted, she caught her breath. They passed under a vine-laden archway and stepped into paradise.

North Star trotted placidly through the most incredible gardens Mariel could have imagined, swishing his tail without much concern, and Gabe too seemed to know the place. But Mariel was beside herself with awe. These gardens rivaled any she'd seen in fancy magazines or gardening books. The winding pathway itself was a true marvel, paved with bricks that, if Mariel weren't mistaken, were real gold. They shimmered in the sunlight and rang beneath the stallion's hooves. Flowers of every variety lined either side, and Mariel found names for only a few of them, including drifts of sunny daffodils, whole patches of irises divided according to color, rows upon rows of stunning tulips, rhododendron bushes, and many more types of flowers Mariel didn't know existed. One section was dedicated entirely to lilies, including the largest lilies Mariel had ever seen, all the way down to tiny dwarf lilies that were mere pixies in comparison.

Wonder after wonder greeted Mariel's wide eyes as they progressed deeper into the gardens. Each delight seemed better than the last, and Mariel gasped in constant amazement. The scent was intoxicating and there were so many butterflies flying around them that they were like jeweled confetti. Mariel's mind whirled. She was almost desperate to touch something. There were tall trees loaded with ripe, reddish-yellow fruits Mariel didn't recognize, and, reaching out, she plucked one from a low branch as they passed and turned it over in her hands, examining it.

Gabe chuckled. "It's a mango, Miss Mariel. Go on, try it."

Mariel needed no second bidding. She was starving, since she'd had no breakfast, and the day had already lengthened into afternoon. She bit into the plump mango and was pleasantly surprised. It tasted much like a tangy peach. Mango juice dribbled down Mariel's chin, much to her embarrassment, and she sheepishly wiped her mouth with her sleeve.

Gabe noticed and grinned. "It's a little bit messy."

Mariel was laughing as she finished the mango in a few hungry bites. All these new experiences were thrilling and so far removed from her small-town upbringing that she couldn't help being giddy. Rosy-cheeked and bright-eyed, feeling like a child wandering in Never-Never Land, she sat up straighter and saw a bearded old man wearing blue overalls and a straw hat stooped over a white rosebush, wielding a pair of pruning shears and clipping away.

North Star drew to a halt of his own accord, and Gabe slid off and held his hands up to Mariel. When she leaned over, he caught her waist and lifted her easily to the ground. The old man straightened and paused in his work to contemplate his visitors. Mariel thought how much he reminded her of some pictures of Father Christmas, because though this man's beard was snow-white, there was something ageless about him. His warm brown eyes were also sparkling and young, and he smiled as she and Gabe approached.

Gabe introduced them. "Miss Mariel Stone, meet the Zookeeper." He bowed.

Uncertain what to do, Mariel awkwardly copied Gabe's example and bowed, also. When Gabe moved towards North Star, Mariel glanced back and was surprised to see that the magnificent white horse had also performed a difficult equine bow, tucking one of his long forelegs and touching his muzzle to the gold bricks. Then he rose to his hooves, and Gabe smiled, waving kindly at Mariel as he led the stallion away.

Mariel turned back to the Zookeeper, clasping her hands expectantly before her. He was regarding her. Mariel gazed back, somehow unafraid in his presence.

"Greetings, Mariel Stone."

Mariel wanted to bow again. "Greetings, Zookeeper."

He smiled warmly at her. "I am pleased that you could come on such short notice."

"Thank you for inviting me, sir."

An amused twinkle appeared in his eyes, as if he would burst out laughing at any moment. "I have heard much about you, daughter."

"Gabe told me something of you, but there was a lot I didn't understand," Mariel admitted. "He told me you would explain everything when I arrived."

The Zookeeper's expression turned to one of joy. "And so I shall, daughter." Holding a satchel in one hand, he held out his other hand to her. "Will you walk with me?"

Mariel nodded and slid her hand into his, finding it not leathery and worn at all, but warm and strong and full of vitality that belied his years. Almost immediately, she loved him as the grandfather she'd never known, though she didn't know why. The old man drew her along the gleaming gold pathway, and Mariel fell into step beside him, gazing up at him with childlike trust.

"You must think these gardens great," he said, sweeping a hand over the living beauty around them. Mariel nodded, and he went on. "Once, long ago, they were much bigger and greater than they are now, filled with all manner of creatures. And now...now it is not so. Now, even the trees miss the birds."

Mariel was surprised to see the deep sadness reflected in his expression, and her heart ached. She wondered if his aging was brought on by sorrow rather than time.

"What happened?" she prompted hesitantly.

He gave a fatherly chuckle, his sadness eclipsed by his obvious attachment to the creatures he spoke of. "Ah, you know how they can be—independent and strong-minded. Especially the younger ones, yes?" He grinned knowingly at Mariel, and with a little blush she smiled back. He was talking about her and she knew it. "They wanted to do things their own way, to live their lives on their own. And I let them. Freedom is the gift I gave them, and they stewarded it wisely, for a time. But then…things changed."

They had taken a detour between stands of grapevines heavy with bunches of purple grapes that made Mariel's mouth water, but the Zookeeper took her past them to an enormous wall of ivy. Then he drew back the vine curtain, revealing an ugly black metal gate with posts thick as pillars spaced mere inches apart.

"Beyond," the old man told her, "is the Other Side. But the trees don't grow half so well, and fewer flowers bloom. Their attempt at building a successful kingdom continually fails. The creatures run amuck like sheep without a shepherd. I hear them complain of it, but they won't allow me inside to fix it."

Mariel leaned her head back to get an idea of how high this gate rose, and its size astonished her. It seemed to divide the sky in two.

"How did they…build this?" she breathed in wonder.

The Zookeeper brushed his hand over the cold metal, his voice full of regret. "Ah, when the will is strong enough, one can accomplish such things. And they did." He sighed, and let the vines slide through his fingers, back into place over the gate.

Mariel was bewildered. "So they just…walled you out, like

that?" He nodded, and Mariel's mind raced. "But isn't there a way to get back in?"

He shook his head. "The same will that built this gate prevents me from returning."

Mariel was beginning to sense the humble leadership the Zookeeper practiced and wished to give to the creatures on the Other Side. "It must be chaos in there," she murmured, staring at the ivy curtain.

The Zookeeper nodded. "It is. And there are a few, a select few, who wish for my return enough to do something about it." He looked at her, and there was a light of hope in his eyes. "That's where you come in, daughter."

Mariel caught her breath as several emotions washed over her—fear, excitement, eagerness and dread. "But…but what can I do that you cannot?" she almost whispered, half in awe and half nervous that someone or something on the Other Side would hear them.

The old man bent and pulled at a bunch of ivy near the ground, concealing a hole that had been bored into one of the massive pillars. "There should be just enough room for you to squeeze through," he said to her. "The creatures that are still fighting made this in hopes of allowing me back inside. It took a long time and a lot of effort, but I can't cross over myself. I must send someone else."

"But…shouldn't Gabe go instead?"

The Zookeeper shook His head. "They know him. They would kill him on sight."

Mariel's blood went cold, and she took a step back. "Will they…try to kill *me*?"

Coming forward, the Zookeeper took her trembling hands in his warm grasp. "Yes, daughter, they will try to kill you," he answered evenly. "But they don't know who you are, and that gives you a chance."

"A very small one," muttered Mariel, biting her lip. She gently drew her hands away and sat down on a boulder beside the little path, overwhelmed.

"You wouldn't be alone, Mariel." The Zookeeper was watching her while she stared at the ground, but it was obvious that he was prepared to accept her decision either way. "Two of my own men, Ralph and Mike, are already hidden inside, doing what they can to help those who still serve me—to the best of their ability. They would help you also."

Mariel turned all this over in her mind, then lifted her eyes to his. "What would I be expected to do?"

The Zookeeper retrieved a tiny worn scroll tied with gold ribbon from a satchel. "This scroll belongs to me," he answered quietly, giving it to her. "It signifies my leadership over the creatures on the Other Side, but they replaced this scroll with one of their own and used it to lock away the key to…the padlock." He waved his hand vaguely towards the wall in an easterly direction. "The padlock cannot be opened without the key. If this scroll were returned to its rightful place, it would release the key, and we could open this gate!" His golden-brown eyes were glimmering as he spoke. "That is a day I have longed for, daughter, very much."

Mariel gazed at the scroll. It was such a small thing, yet it was everything. It was as if she held all the dearest hopes of the Zookeeper in her hands. And the dearest hopes of the Zookeeper revolved not around himself, but on the creatures he loved and missed greatly. She looked around at the stunning gardens and noticed for the first time that there was an aura of sadness which the great beauty disguised. Knowing the heart of the Zookeeper revealed also the secrets of his garden.

Her eyes traveled to the path and back the way she'd come. She thought over the incredible journey with Gabe on North Star, and it seemed a tragedy to waste all that effort. Besides, knowing what she knew now, how could she turn her back on the Zookeeper? Seeing what she had seen, how could she go home and be content with pretending it never happened, or letting it fade to simple memory?

Exhaling shakily, Mariel closed her fingers over the scroll. "I will go, Zookeeper."

Joy bright as a sunrise shone in the old man's eyes, and he smiled. "Thank you, daughter."

Recovering a little of her wry wit, Mariel managed a grin. "Don't thank me yet, sir."

The Zookeeper tilted back his head and laughed, and the flowers and the butterflies danced at the sound of it. Mariel joined his infectious mirth and stood up, filled with greater courage now that she'd accepted her mission. She tucked the scroll away in her jeans' pocket.

The Zookeeper pressed her hand. "Keep your eyes open for a friendly creature somewhere nearby," he advised. "This scroll had been kept on the Other Side in a highly secure location, but it was stolen and passed through that hole, so I would find it. Someone will be watching for my messenger, hoping for your arrival." Then he set his hands gently on her forehead. "My blessing be upon you, daughter."

Mariel moved towards the wall and drew back the ivy, then paused for one last look around the garden. It was all so beautiful, so peaceful…so full of life. It was the kind of place she'd always dreamed of finding. Now that she'd found it—or had been brought to it—she was leaving it behind for uncertainty and danger. She wondered if she would ever see it, or anything familiar, again.

Taking a deep breath, Mariel smiled bravely at the Zookeeper, dropped to the ground, and wriggled through the narrow opening to the Other Side.

CHAPTER
FIVE

The Other Side looked so dull and colorless compared with the Zookeeper's gardens that Mariel sat for a while in the dried grass and let her senses readjust. The undulating gray-green hills before her showed no sign of life, but there was a faint outline of an ancient rutted road leading away from the black gate. It was obviously little-used, and Mariel wondered if the other end of that trail led to nowhere in much the same manner.

There was only one way to find out.

Rising, Mariel set off. If she was in for a lot of walking, she might as well get started, though the hot July sun made for a miserable afternoon journey. When she reached the foot of the broken road, she found that time had weathered the bricks away, leaving little or no evidence of its having been there once—just a few broken stones scattered here and there. But there were enough to follow.

After hours of steady tramping, a weary Mariel was beginning to wonder if the road led anywhere at all. It was late afternoon and her feet were killing her. Looking back, she found the empty hills she'd left behind, and before her were more empty hills that seemed exactly the same. Mariel chewed her lip worriedly and squinted against the sun's merciless glare. She was already hungry, and thirst was taking its toll on her, and now she was tired and sweaty as well. No wonder vultures were wheeling in the washed-out blue sky.

Mariel made a face at the grotesque birds. There were five or six of them. "I don't recommend coming down here," she muttered, swallowing hard in her parched throat. "I'm hungry enough to *eat* one of you. Maybe two."

Perhaps Mariel's threat worked. The vultures rose to a higher orbit, wheeling in wider and wider circles as if their focus had shifted away from the lone girl. It was one small victory for Mariel, and she drew on that sense of satisfaction to keep going. She had no intention of ending up as a prospective meal for the buzzards.

Mariel went on and on and on, letting her eyelids fall to half-mast. Her angry stomach collaborated with her imagination to conjure whole feasts of cheeseburgers with huge baskets of fries and extra-large milkshakes, or massive slices of pepperoni pizza fairly dripping with melted cheese, or buckets of fried chicken with mashed potatoes and buttered biscuits drowned in brown gravy; and a parade of pies ranging from apple to pumpkin floated before her dazed vision. She guessed she'd doggedly covered at least ten miles of intermittent pathway by now. Still the stubborn scenery remained the same—gray-green hills uninhabited by sentient beings. Even the buzzards had abandoned her, and Mariel added loneliness to her growing list of complaints.

Another hour or so later, conditions hadn't improved at all. It was all Mariel could do to focus on placing one aching and heavy foot in front of the other. The sun was headed westward, but it beat down on her as hot as ever. Mariel felt faint enough that she wondered if the little cluster of brick buildings growing awkwardly out of the distant horizon was a mirage. She kept waiting for them to vanish in the wavering heat as she drew closer.

Instead, the details of the buildings grew sharper. The road meandering between the structures was in far better repair than the section Mariel was currently walking, and a variety of animals—Mariel could just make out a Holstein cow, a zebra and two turkeys—wandered around outside. There was a little bridge with a sign Mariel couldn't yet read and, if she weren't mistaken…the soft splashing of a gentle stream.

A thought struck: Mirages weren't accompanied by sound. Water! Mariel broke into a half-stumbling run, leaving the path and rushing the last few hundred yards with no eyes for anything but the gushing black water. She fell to her knees beside the peaceful stream, plunging her face gratefully into the cool liquid. The shock of it was delightfully invigorating. Life returned to her worn-out soul. Mariel drew back and, cupping her hands to capture little pools, she drank the water with a will.

Only when her terrific thirst had been satiated did she notice the rippling reflection of animals watching her in the stream. With a little cry she sat back suddenly, blinking at a fat donkey with spots on his muzzle and the moppy little lapdog with a red bow in her fur beside him. Immediately, Mariel wondered if these were creatures friendly to the Zookeeper—and rather hoped not. They were a strange pair. The donkey shook his large head and blew his scraggly white forelock out of his eyes.

"Do you believe it, Jo? Do you believe it?" he muttered aside to the lapdog, watching Mariel but seeming to look through her.

The lapdog, Jo, gave Mariel a little canine smirk and yipped. "Gracious, child, you must have been thirsty," she said.

"Er…yes, a little," stammered Mariel, climbing awkwardly to her aching feet and brushing off her shirt in an attempt to look more presentable.

"Hm. Well, now I'm thirsty." She turned her head up to the donkey. "I'm thirsty, Teddy," she pouted with a little whine, pawing at his knee.

"Mff." The donkey shook her away absently. "Can you swim?"

Jo cocked her head in puzzlement and yipped again. "Can I swim? What do you mean, Teddy?"

The old donkey stomped a lazy hoof. "Oh, nothin' really, just wonderin'."

Utterly bewildered by then, Mariel pulled back her sopping hair into a ponytail and squeezed out a stream of water. "Where am I?" she asked, coming towards the bridge.

"Can't you read, child?" wondered Jo, glancing from the girl to the large sign Mariel had seen from far away. Up close now, Mariel read: *Welcome to The Menagerie!* A smaller sign tacked beneath it stated: *Pardon our dust. Under renovation.*

"The Menagerie?" repeated Mariel. "What's that?"

"Buh," mumbled Teddy, flapping his wispy tail. Then he

heaved a deep sigh, staring down past his hooves to the flowing water below. "Where am I, where am I?"

Jo yipped and addressed Mariel. "You're here, aren't you? You might as well find out for yourself what the Menagerie is like." Without further explanation, the lapdog turned on her donkey companion, ignoring his mutterings. "I'm still thirsty, Teddy."

Convinced these two were quite out of their minds, Mariel stepped onto the bridge and edged past them as their argument continued.

"Coke and a rum, coke and a rum," sighed the donkey. "Was it two or three?"

Yip! Yip! Yip! Jo hopped about in agitation. "I don't know, I think it was more, but I'm still thirsty!"

Not sure exactly what she'd just witnessed, Mariel was glad to leave the bridge behind. She passed through an unmanned golden gate, which was already open, and seemed more decorative than functional, and entered a bustling little metropolis filled with a diverse variety of animals. The buildings were made of red brick, Mariel could see now, and set tightly together. The Holstein cow mooed at Mariel, and went back to grazing. The zebra and the turkeys ignored her. The path wound through the middle of town and grew steep, rising and falling sharply. Mariel laboriously climbed her way to the top of the first hill and heard a soft splash behind her. Looking back at the bridge, she noticed the donkey and the lapdog were gone.

"They must have decided to go for a swim," muttered Mariel, frowning and shaking her head. Then she turned away and passed deeper into the Menagerie.

A huge panda sat outside one of the buildings, placidly munching stalks of bamboo. Mariel was tempted to ask him for some, but bamboo was not exactly a cheeseburger, so she refrained and went looking for something else. The air was full of other tantalizing smells. Mariel got caught behind a slow-moving parade of sleepy otters wearing *Save the Whales* buttons, and rather impatiently the girl moved out of line and passed them, pausing when she noticed a stand where a grinning Siberian tiger was selling hot dogs.

"Good afternoon," said the tiger with a low bow of his head.

Mariel was almost too hungry to answer. She fumbled in her jeans' pocket and set a few bills on the counter, earning her a pair of mustard-covered corn dogs. Those vanished almost instantly, and with a final gulp Mariel smiled gratefully at the tiger.

"Thank you. Those were the best corn dogs I've had in my entire life," she said.

The tiger bowed again, grinning and making no reply to that, which Mariel found odd. She tossed her corn-dog sticks in a nearby trash can and wandered down the street at a more relaxed pace, happy to have something in her stomach.

She was soon caught in another parade again—this time made up of large predatory cats, primarily cheetahs and panthers, all wearing *Save the Penguins* collars. Mariel was possessed by curiosity. A fellow dressed all in khaki like a zoo ranger was tossing a bucketful of silver fish to a pack of eager seals, and Mariel stepped aside to have a word with him.

"Excuse me," Mariel began politely, trying not to think about raw fish when she'd just consumed corn dogs. "Can you tell me why those animals are picketing?"

"You want the low-down? Sure thing, dude," answered the well-tanned young man, grinning amiably at Mariel as if he'd known her all his life. "It's all about the politics, dude, 'cause, like, if otters are busy savin' the whales, nobody cares if they eat the little fish, you know?" He chuckled, his half-lidded gaze wandering over the crowd of barking seals. "Same thing with, like, the panthers and their bird-habits. Gotta save the penguins for the sake of the ol' image."

"Oh." That explanation rather defeated Mariel's logic, and she brushed strands of clinging wet hair that had fallen loose from her ponytail out of her face as she rejoined the crowded street that was now populated by a whole procession of raccoons devoted to preserving the alligator. Still famished, she stopped by a cart run by a friendly beaver and purchased a basket of breaded shrimp. She munched these as she continued along the hilly path, tossing the shrimp tails to the flocks of pigeons and seagulls that drifted in her wake.

Abruptly, Mariel became aware that birds weren't the only creatures following her. From the corner of her eye, she caught a movement of an animal she couldn't readily identify darting into the shadows between two buildings. Mariel gulped, quickening her pace, pretending to have her attention caught by a souvenir stand in order to cast a surreptitious glance over her shoulder. Her shadow was still following.

Fear gripped her. Had someone seen her entering from the Zookeeper's gate? She recalled the vultures whirling overhead against the watery sun; how long had they been up there before she noticed them? Could they have been spies?

She was nearing a less populated section of the Menagerie, and Mariel scanned the road ahead to see the buildings rapidly thinning. Very soon, she would leave behind the last of the crowds and find herself alone. There were no side trails to take, and she couldn't go back, or she'd run straight into her unknown pursuer. Mariel's mind raced. She was running out of options fast.

Taking a desperate chance, she suddenly whirled and flung the remaining shrimp in her basket all over the path. The birds went mad with glee, flapping and fighting and screeching over the unexpected feast. Mariel broke into a run and darted inside one of the buildings, pressing herself against the doorway and hoping her diversion had worked. She waited in the dark, her heart pounding as she listened to the avian cacophony.

The shrimp battle died down when the last crumbs vanished, which didn't take long. Shortly Mariel would be discovered if she loitered there, and she looked around in desperation.

Luck was with her. The building she'd chosen to hide in was busy with activity. Light spilled out of the archway, and beyond, something was happening. A great many people and creatures were cheering, clapping, roaring, barking and shouting. Curious about the commotion and still hoping to escape her shadow, she moved through the archway and found herself in an arena of some kind, standing in the upper balconies. Below, a blue-matted boxing ring with a lone zebra was the center of attention. A fat walrus wearing a ridiculously little black bowler stopped Mariel, holding out a flipper.

"Just a minute, miss. Where's your ticket?"

Mariel groaned and dug through her pockets, producing the last few dollar bills she'd brought with her. The walrus promptly tore off a ticket and handed it to her.

"Enjoy the show, miss," he boomed, chuffing as he himself turned to gaze down at the boxing ring.

Mariel didn't ask questions. With one last nervous glance at the doorway, she hurried into the stands and found a seat she thought would be relatively inconspicuous, as she was sandwiched in between a fat llama and a baby elephant. Both were making a lot of noise—especially the baby elephant, who was trumpeting away, even though the contestants had not yet arrived in the ring.

Mariel looked anxiously towards the ticket table. The walrus was speaking with someone, but Mariel couldn't see who.

Assorted animals were blocking her view. Swallowing hard, she picked up a discarded red-and-white candy-striped bucket, now empty of popcorn, and flipped the greasy container over her head.

The llama noticed and gave her a strange look. Thinking fast, Mariel leaped to her feet, hollering at the top of her lungs.

"Let's go, let's go!" she shouted, clapping her hands like a truly rabid fan. Then she took her seat again, feigning eagerness for the match to begin, while in truth her straining from left to right was a vain attempt for a better look at whoever was getting the ticket from the walrus.

Just as a deafening roar from the crowd announced the entrance of the boxers, Mariel spotted a large black wolf pacing into the stands, carrying a ticket in his mouth and obviously looking for someone.

CHAPTER
SIX

Instinctively Mariel hunkered down in her seat and nearly got her foot stepped on by the excited baby elephant. She moved it aside just in time. The entire arena burst into an uproar as two kangaroos—one wearing red gloves, long red shoes and a red foam helmet, while the other sported blue gear—sprang from their respective locker rooms and bounded between the ropes into the ring. Mariel ignored their bouncing around and mock punches at the air; she'd lost sight of the black wolf in all the commotion, and that worried her. The creature could be anywhere and Mariel was certain it had come for her.

The cream-colored llama was watching her again. "Looking for someone?" asked the kindly female.

"Er, no!" Mariel forced a smile, but her stomach was roiling with anxiety. "This is just…so exciting. I can't wait 'til it starts."

Drawing the popcorn bucket lower over her forehead, Mariel did her best to act the part of a sports-crazy teenager, all the while casting glances through the crowd for the wolf, who seemingly disappeared without a trace. That really bothered Mariel. She felt as if he could be anywhere, watching her. His yellow eyes seemed to peer out from every shadow, between every knot of animals. For pretense's sake, she shouted and clapped and decided to cheer for the red kangaroo, a decision partially aided by the baby elephant's obvious favorite.

"Go Red!" Her cry, while exuberant enough, sounded half-hearted in her own ears. Mariel glanced at the llama. The knowing look in the fluffy mammal's brown eyes told Mariel that she hadn't fooled her, either.

"Come here often?"

The coy tone was a warning to Mariel. There was something of a trap in those words, but since Mariel didn't know much about Menagerie sports customs, she didn't know what it was. It would be only too easy to make a fatal mistake and give herself away. Mariel smiled, though she was feeling sick, and adopted Beth's habits as best she could. She squirreled around in her seat and chewed at her nails.

"As often as life permits," she hazarded.

"Oh, yes?" Mariel had the distinctively uncomfortable impression that the llama was toying with her. "Do you usually sit in the upper deck?"

Mariel was done for and she knew it. Hoping for a clue to the right answer, she swept a desperate glance over the lower part of the arena and noticed that the spectators down there were mostly comprised of elephants and donkeys, segregated distinctly by race and favorite. The elephants were rooting for the red kangaroo while the donkeys cheered on the blue side, waving pennants and wearing buttons or collars in their favorite contestant's color. A few bald eagles were scattered throughout both groups, along with various other animals—a grizzly bear, a beaver, a puma, and a great big bull Mariel recognized as a Texas longhorn among them. There were hardly any humans, so far as Mariel could tell.

"Um…most of the time," she muttered aside to the llama, half-hoping her voice would be lost in the shouting—or that the llama would have lost interest in the girl by now.

There was no chance of the latter, Mariel saw to her great dismay. The llama had lost interest in the boxing match instead, which began at the clang of a bell and a roar from the audience. Muffled thumping could be heard over the din as the kangaroos pummeled each other—mostly with their enormous feet. They reared backwards, balancing on their tails, and pounded away in a most amusing manner.

Mariel wasn't concentrating either. She couldn't even act intrigued by the match anymore. The pressure of having a wolf following her coupled with the llama asking probing questions was too much for her fragile nerves. The chewing of her fingernails became less an imitation of Beth and more a real sign of fear.

"So you do sit down there sometimes?" pressed the llama.

Mariel stiffened. Then she pretended she was too absorbed in the activities below to have heard the llama.

"You've never been here before, have you?"

Mariel cleared her throat and backtracked. "Mostly I sit up here, but I've been down there on occasion."

"Interesting." Mariel strained her ears to catch the woolly animal's quiet speech. "Only the highly privileged sit down there. Once it was that they had to be chosen fairly, but now they buy their own tickets."

Mariel froze.

The llama gave a soft, lilting laugh and set her muzzle against Mariel's shoulder. "Don't be afraid, little one. You are safe with me." Mariel swallowed hard. Despite her kind words, Mariel couldn't bear to look at her. The noise of the arena faded into the background.

"Who are you?" whispered the girl.

"My name is Anna," came the reply, "and as you can see, I'm…a llama." She broke off with another quiet laugh.

Mariel dared risk a sideways glance and found nothing but honesty in Anna's gentle face. She was also quite old, Mariel realized with a start, but the llama's brown eyes were startlingly clear and comprehending. She favored Mariel with a warm knowing look.

"Your pursuer has gone for now," she assured the girl quietly, ignoring Mariel's scowl of distress. "He wouldn't attack you in a public place like this—yet. Though things are steadily changing for the worse." Anna sighed, looking tired and somehow older, as if she carried a terrible weight on her shoulders. "Stay with me, and I will see that you aren't left alone again and vulnerable to your enemies."

"My enemies!" Mariel hissed. The tension building inside her exploded—this llama seemed to know everything. Mariel wasn't sure how and she worried she'd betrayed herself somehow. "Listen, I really don't need your help, thank you. I can handle my—"

Suddenly, they were interrupted by a loud, trumpeting blast from the exuberant baby elephant, who was bouncing up and down in his chair. It creaked ominously beneath the huge calf's weight. "Red-Red-Red! Get 'im, Red! Don't let 'im…oh, no, not again!" He flapped his enormous ears over his eyes as if he couldn't watch anymore.

Mariel focused her attention on the match. The red kangaroo had been knocked flat on his rump, his huge feet sticking up as he sat there, looking at the zebra imploringly. Scattered cries of, "That was a low blow, ref!" rippled through the arena, and it added to the wronged kangaroo's plea.

But the zebra was unmoved. Stamping his forehooves decisively, he blew a blast on his whistle. "Ready, and…fight!" He shifted to one side, leaving the kangaroos unobstructed.

Red barely had time to scramble to his feet before he was nearly buried under an onslaught of rough blows from Blue. Ducking and stumbling backwards, Red was forced against the ropes, managing a few weak punches against Blue's ribcage. Suddenly Mariel was on her feet, shouting at the top of her lungs with the rest. It was no longer a pretense.

"Don't let 'im take you down, Red! Brace your tail and—"

Red was already doing just that, and he leveraged a mighty thump with his blue-padded feet that sent Blue skidding to the opposite side of the ring. The elephant peered cautiously over his ear, then fluttered the ears away from his eyes and blasted joyously with his trunk. Mariel unleashed a wild holler of delight and applauded until teeth clamped down on her back pocket and jerked the girl into her seat.

"Don't draw too much attention to yourself," advised Anna, her whiskery lips tickling Mariel's ear. "We're still being watched, remember?"

Mariel emerged from the emotion of the fight immediately. She had much more important things to worry about than a boxing match. The bell sounded just then, mercifully giving Red the chance to sit in his corner and regroup. Blue did the same, and Mariel had never seen a kangaroo look so smug.

"What do I do?" Mariel whispered back, deciding to trust Anna. She didn't have a choice. The llama knew about her mission, to some degree, and Mariel had no one else to turn to.

"Wait," was Anna's soft reply. "When the first wave of spectators departs after this match is over, we leave with them." Turning aside, the llama scanned the rafters until she spotted a young pigeon, and Anna blinked her thick-lashed eyes four times. The pigeon gave a momentary expression of utter shock until Anna repeated the sign, then the bird all but fell off its perch and flapped madly out of the building.

Noticing Mariel staring after the bird, Anna gave a placid smile. "We've waited for you a long time, little one. But I'll tell you more later," she added quickly, seeing the girl's heightened interest. "We can't talk here…about anything except boxing."

Mariel's curiosity was not easily assuaged, but it could be diverted. She turned her attention to the spectators, especially the ones below, just as the bell sounded and the kangaroos bounded towards each other, thumping away with their big feet. "Who are they, and why is it such a big deal to sit down there?" she murmured aside to the llama.

"The rich are there, now," Anna replied, pointing out one portly donkey in particular. "See him? He's notorious for paying off the zebras. He's on the blue side, of course."

"Well…" Mariel was indignant. "Why doesn't someone stop him? Aren't there committees in place for this sort of flagrant violation of conduct?"

Anna chuffed. "Oh, there are, dearie, but he's paid them off too."

Mariel's blue eyes blazed. "What's the world coming to?"

"I ask myself the same question every day," replied the llama softly, just as Red landed a hard punch to his opponent and knocked him out. The zebra blew a blast on his whistle, checked the unconscious Blue over carefully, and—it seemed

56

to Mariel—grudgingly declared Red the winner, which brought a roar from the Red side and a disgruntled murmuring from the Blue section. The portly donkey glared at the zebra, who shrugged.

Anna smiled. "But sometimes, sometimes the right side still prevails. Now come."

Mariel cringed and covered her ears from the noise of the baby elephant's jubilant celebration, and she got up and hurried after the llama, along with a knot of chattering creatures all heading for the exit. Mariel cast surreptitious glances around for the wolf and didn't see him. Anna looked neither right nor left as she led the way past the ticketing walrus and out into the late afternoon sunshine.

Mariel was surprised to find it was still daylight. The day's events had been exhausting, and she was more than ready to put her head on a pillow and hibernate. Her weariness was evident in her shuffling walk, but Anna didn't seem to notice. She was leading the way towards a large dappled-gray workhorse with a young pigeon perched on his thick-maned neck. Mariel recognized the pigeon as the same one who'd left the building shortly before.

The horse snorted and lifted a white-feathered hoof to paw impatiently when he saw Anna. He cast a measuring glance over Mariel, and a little light of hope sprang into his dull eyes. He shook his head, and his forelock fell askew over his white-whiskered muzzle. "Greetings, servant of the master," he said in a low, rumbling tone. "What is your name?"

Mariel saw no reason to hide it. "Er...Mariel. Mariel Stone."

"Mariel Stone," mused Simeon, a smile twitching at his muzzle.

Anna quickened her trot. "Simeon, let's go." She went down the hilly path without waiting for him to catch up.

Simeon gave Mariel a kindly smile as she came up beside him, and they moved after Anna in companionable silence. Simeon waited until they were in a valley before making an offer Mariel couldn't refuse in her sore-footed condition: a horseback ride.

"My old bones can't take much these days," said the great horse, chuckling, "but I dare say, you are a little human-foal still, and you ought to be a feather in comparison with the plow. Scramble aboard."

This was easier said than done, and Simeon had to stand beside a large boulder just so Mariel could get high enough off the ground to settle onto the giant animal's back. Simeon set off at a plodding trot. His hooves were the size of dinner plates, and his walk was rather jarring, but Mariel was too tired to care and too polite to complain. Anna murmured softly in conversation with Simeon, and their voices were so low that Mariel couldn't tell if they were speaking her language or an animal tongue she could never have deciphered.

Mariel still worried because they knew so much about her, but there was nothing to be done about that now. She had to risk trusting them. Their quiet murmurings were still beyond her hearing or understanding, but little by little, the need for sleep overcame her. As their journey progressed, the weary girl leaned down over Simeon's neck, settled her head into his coarse gray mane, and fell fast asleep while the pigeon watched over her.

CHAPTER SEVEN

Mariel had the strangest sensation while she slept—as if she were falling, slowly, without the slightest fear. Something soft caught her, and with a tired moan, she rolled onto her side and snuggled into it, giving into unconsciousness once more.

When she woke up, she had no idea where she was. She lay still, blinking, her bleary eyes slowly drifting over the old wooden beams that made up the rafters. The pungent odors around her reminded her of animals and musty hay, and she realized...she was lying *in* a pile of hay.

With a start Mariel sat up. A bit of tattered cloth she hadn't noticed before slipped to her waist—a makeshift blanket. She'd spent the night in a barn.

Soft chuckling drew the girl's attention, and she whirled to find Anna the llama standing nearby, watching her. "Good morning, sleepy one. I thought you'd sleep forever."

"Not even Rip Van Winkle could accomplish *that* feat," Mariel responded wryly, picking bits of straw from her unruly hair.

Anna cocked her head quizzically. "Who's Rip Van Winkle?"

"Never mind," Mariel sighed, climbing to her still-aching feet. She was not in the mood to answer pointless questions—not when she had so many questions of her own. "Where am I?"

"In a stable beyond the city limits," Anna responded, unruffled by Mariel's morning crankiness. She idly jigged a hoof up and down, and a fleeting expression of sadness passed over her features. "Simeon and I live here, among others like us. But more questions will keep for later. I imagine you're hungry."

Mariel gulped. That was an understatement. Wordlessly, she followed the llama into the soft sunshine, where a glorious sight met Mariel's eyes. A table, covered in a gold tablecloth, was spread with delicious things in wide variety and great quantity.

Mariel's questions vanished. Eagerly, she scrambled into one of the large chairs, tucked a napkin onto her lap, and seized the fork with every intention of digging immediately into the nearest dish, which happened to be a plate loaded with strawberry pancakes and smothered in whipped cream.

"Just a moment, dear," bid the llama, much to Mariel's dismay. The smell was making her mouth water. "We have to wait for the others."

Fortunately, Mariel was not obliged to wait long. Other creatures emerged from the stable in a long procession. Leading the way was old Simeon himself, a pleased smile on his white-whiskered muzzle, as he plodded up to the great table. The pigeon rode on his neck. Behind them came a small herd of sheep, a gloriously beautiful white swan, and a knot of very small creatures: rabbits, squirrels, chipmunks, even a mouse who didn't seem at all afraid of the calico cat. Mariel watched in perplexed awe as they surrounded the table. Very few of them needed chairs—or could use them at all—so the majority of them stood for their meals or sat on the table itself, next to plates of food that outdid the littlest ones in size. The squirrels and the chipmunks worked in tandem to tug a plate of cream-colored walnut pudding to one side, so they could eat it in peace.

But nobody touched their food; they all seemed to be waiting for something.

The pigeon fluttered away from the horse and alighted beside Mariel, giving her a little avian smile, which she slowly returned. Being amidst an enchanted animal kingdom such as this one was the stuff of dreams, but Mariel was slowly accepting it as reality.

At last Simeon lowered his great head, and all the creatures did likewise. Mariel uncertainly clasped her hands and joined them.

"We thank you, Master, for providing this day's fodder," the ancient workhorse was saying, "and we pray that one day, we will see you again."

That was that. Everyone sent up a small cheer, and they eagerly plunged in, and Mariel along with them. They'd barely begun to nibble at their breakfast when suddenly the pigeon gave a short chirp of alarm, and all heads jerked heavenwards. A tiny black dot that Mariel recognized as a bird could be seen flying in the distance.

"The crows! The crows!" And just like that, there was a mad scramble of creatures leaping from the table and into the grass, and they made a rapid dash for the barn. Mariel crouched down in alarm and slunk off her chair, and strong teeth gripped her shirt sleeve as she began to run, forcing her to move faster. Glancing sideways as she hurried along, Mariel found Anna beside her, holding her sleeve, and Simeon was right behind her. Anna pushed Mariel into the stable and came in after her. Last of all, Simeon charged to safety, his broad shoulder slamming into Mariel. Anna released her arm and the girl toppled backwards, landing hard on the stable floor.

Mariel clapped a hand over her mouth and didn't dare cry out. She remained where she'd fallen and peered out from behind the workhorse's enormous hooves. Everyone was holding a collective breath. Mariel counted her heartbeats until, in a flapping of feathers, a black bird descended from the sky and landed on the back of the chair Mariel had been sitting in. The bird shook himself off, coughing.

"Ugh! I hate soot!"

Simeon's head poked out of the barn doorway. "Marcus?"

Flapping his wings in sheer irritation and raising a cloud of black dust, Marcus tossed a glance at the stable. "Jeez, tell everyone to come out already. I'm not gonna eat anybody, but I *am* gonna eat somebody's breakfast if—"

A stampede of animals cut him off as they all raced back to the table. Mariel picked herself off the ground, brushing off her jeans and looking completely bewildered. Anna was entirely relaxed, and Simeon fearlessly stepped out into the sunshine.

"You know, Marc, you could have ditched the soot disguise *before* you got here."

"What, and take a bath?" The bird shuddered violently. Marcus entirely ignored the moaning chorus of disgust from nearby creatures who found themselves showered with black dust. "I'd have lost time. Wet feathers are bad for flight."

Desperate curiosity and roaring hunger were getting the best of Mariel, and she cautiously edged up to Simeon and peered over the giant gray horse to have a look at the bird herself. He was certainly the strangest-looking crow she'd ever seen, with a slightly longer neck and a rounder beak. As some of the soot loosened and fell away, Mariel recognized a seagull beneath the black powder.

Behind her, Anna chuckled. "That's Marcus. He's one of ours, and he's back from a little mission we had for him. He had to disguise himself as one of *them* in order to remain undetected."

"So why did *we* run for cover then?" asked Mariel. "Is eating breakfast illegal? Never mind, don't answer that." The other animals were already eating, and Mariel went running back to her chair and sat down, glancing up at the seagull perched over her. "Hello, Marcus. If you don't mind, I'm going to sit here and have a bit of food before I starve to death. Kindly refrain from flapping soot into my breakfast, thank you. It interferes with my digestion." She tempered her words with a well-meaning smile.

Marcus didn't seem to take offense and hopped off the chair, fluttering to the ground. There he resumed his attempts at shedding his false coloration. Mariel ignored him then in favor of sustenance, and she picked up her fork with a will. So absorbed was the girl in her delicious meal that she hardly noticed Simeon and Anna returning to the table with slightly worried expressions, and Marcus had disappeared. Only after

Mariel had eliminated every last trace of the strawberry pancakes did she look around for more and notice what her companions were dining on.

The rabbit was eating some dish unfamiliar to Mariel, but it looked rather like green jello with fresh pink clover buds protruding from it. The cat stood on her chair, her forepaws braced on the table as she munched delicately at a helping of scrambled eggs. The sheep were thoroughly enjoying blueberry-and-apple muffins, and the swan pecked at a mound of biscuits.

Mariel was almost too fascinated to eat any more, but the temptation of a cherry crepe overrode her curiosity for a while, and she tucked it away—along with hash browns, a cinnamon roll dripping with cream cheese frosting, and two juicy clementines. Everything was so delicious that Mariel was disappointed when she couldn't eat another bite.

Sitting back, she wiped her fingertips delicately on the napkin. Anna and Simeon had already finished and were watching her, obviously concerned.

"What's with the long faces?" wondered Mariel.

"We've received news," replied Simeon gravely. "Our messenger found—"

He was interrupted by a lot of splashing from the water trough. Mariel whirled and saw Marcus taking a bath, vigorously shaking his feathers and slowly becoming a white and gray seagull again. Mariel made a face and hopped off her chair, and Anna and Simeon led the way into the barn where they could talk in peace.

"We sent Marcus as a messenger to find out about obtaining the key, so we could let the Zookeeper back into the Menagerie," explained Simeon, whisking his tail in a worried manner. "But we ran into a few problems. First of all, the real scroll that had been there before—the one containing the

Rules of Freedom—has been replaced. Instead, there is a facsimile called the Rules of Free Will in its place."

"What's the difference?" Mariel wanted to know. "They sound the same to me."

"They were meant to," Anna replied, shaking her long, fluffy neck. "The Rules of Freedom were written by the Zookeeper, but some creatures decided it was too restricting. So they wrote the Rules of Free Will and convinced a great percentage of the Menagerie that their scroll was new and improved, giving everyone *more* freedom than the Zookeeper had to offer."

"But it didn't?" guessed Mariel, folding her arms and glancing between the two animals.

Simeon chuffed. "No. It shut the Zookeeper out of the Menagerie, and we've been on a slippery slope since then. That's why we stole the Rules of Freedom scroll, with a lot of difficulty, and slipped it through the black gate. That's the scroll you now carry. As some of us predicted, without the original scroll in place, everything has fallen apart."

Mariel frowned thoughtfully. "What exactly has gone wrong?"

"What hasn't," sighed Anna, casting her eyes heavenward.

Simeon pawed moodily at the hay-covered floor. "I think the best way to answer that question is to show you."

With a gasp, Anna whirled towards Simeon. "Are you sure that's a good idea?"

Simeon's expression was equally dour. "Things are not too far gone just yet, and they don't know why she's here. I think we'll be safe enough."

"I don't think I would risk it," put in Anna doubtfully.

"She has to go that way to get to the Capital, Anna."

Mariel tentatively broke in, "Are…the vultures trustworthy?"

Horse and llama heads shifted towards the girl. "Some of them are all right," Simeon answered slowly. "But they gossip terribly, and the majority supports the other side. Why?"

"Because…vultures were circling in the sky when I entered the Menagerie."

A silence fell. Simeon resumed pawing at the hay, and Anna looked out the door, at a loss for words. Outside, lambs were playing a game of tag, and the swan was strolling serenely across the yard. Mariel didn't see how it happened, but their breakfast dishes had been cleared away and the table was gone.

At last Mariel spoke up. "You know, I want to see this for myself."

Simeon cocked an ear in her direction. "Any particular reason why?"

"Because the Zookeeper commissioned me for this," she answered with more boldness than she felt. "Danger has already shadowed my steps. But I'll never get anywhere if I stay here, and I'll have to pass through that part of the Menagerie anyway if I am to reach my destination. You said so yourself, Simeon." Horse and llama were staring at her, somewhat slack-jawed, but Mariel's thoughts continued without them. "Speaking of which, do you happen to have a map?"

Anna slowly nodded, backing away. "Yes, I'll…go get it…" Stumbling over her own hooves, she whirled and trotted off to one of the supply rooms.

Simeon's gaze gentled to one of admiration. "You're a very brave girl."

Sighing, Mariel shook her head. "I wish that were true."

CHAPTER EIGHT

After another very filling breakfast the following morning, Mariel was surprised to find she didn't want to leave the barn. Reluctantly she shouldered the pack Anna had given her, which was full of food and a few miscellaneous supplies such as rope and a map of the Menagerie.

Beside her, Anna noted the girl's wistful look. "Ready to go?"

Slowly, Mariel nodded. "Yeah, I guess. I just…for the first time, I understand how a barn-sour horse feels."

Simeon chuckled good-naturedly. "Watch your comments in regards to animals in the Menagerie," he advised.

Mariel flushed, suddenly remembering that one of her companions was a horse. She gave him a sheepish smile, and the little party of three set off.

Looking back now, Mariel saw their location in hindsight for the first time. The barn was situated well outside the city limits, nestled in rolling gray-green hills. Far in the distance, Mariel could pick out the tall shapes of skyscrapers and the dome of the sporting arena. Shifting her pack against her shoulder, Mariel trotted up to Anna's side.

"I was wondering. Why do you live so far from civilization?"

The llama's placid expression turned to one of weariness. "The city is changing, little one," she responded with a sigh. "You've seen part of it already—the corruption, the misuse of power, the foul play. More and more, it's not only becoming commonplace, but it's being viewed as normality."

Mariel was aghast. "Why would anyone in their right minds—"

"Because they're not in their right minds," Anna interrupted calmly. "It can be argued that if success is the goal, and not integrity towards one's fellow creatures, then they are doing what they believe is right."

"But it's wrong," argued Mariel, scowling.

"Depends on your point of view," returned the llama neutrally. Then she smiled and turned her head towards the girl. "It is indeed wrong, though."

Mariel's mind was in a whirl of furious thought. "But surely they can be made to see the truth, Anna."

The llama kicked at a loose rock in the road, then glanced

behind her at the diminishing barn in the distance. "One would hope, little one. But what benefit is there to serving one's fellow creatures, when one can serve oneself and reap a much greater personal reward?" Anna's head swiveled back towards Mariel. "This is one major reason society deteriorates rapidly without…without the Master. Those who choose to follow that path will stop at nothing to obtain wealth and power and selfish gain. They'll run over anyone who gets in their way."

"Then they should be stopped," put in Mariel.

"Mm-hm."

"Someone should fight them."

The llama nodded. "I agree."

Mariel stopped in her tracks, staring at her companion. "Then why don't you?"

Anna trotted around to face her, and Simeon plodded up to them, his ears pricked with interest. Anna nodded towards the workhorse. "Look at us, little one. We're not so young anymore."

"But surely there is still something you can do," said the girl, looking earnestly from one to the other. "Hiding in a barn in the rural countryside isn't going to improve life for you or anyone else."

Simeon chuckled softly and shook his forelock out of his eyes. "On the contrary. That barn is a haven for those who still follow the Master," he answered in his deep, gentle voice. "Not all of them can survive in the city. Not every creature was born to fight on the front lines. Armies consist of captains, foot soldiers, and those who manufacture supplies. We are in one of the latter roles. We…we support those who live on the front lines in every way we can."

Mariel looked doubtful. "Does it really make a difference?"

Anna smiled placidly. "We're making a difference for you,

child. And you have the most important mission of all, and we…" Her soft brown eyes flicked to Simeon, then back to the girl. "We've waited a long time for the Ambassador of Freedom the Zookeeper said He would send us. You are our life's mission."

Simeon nodded in agreement.

Mariel was stunned into silence. Her hand strayed to the jeans' pocket where she carried the tiny scroll—and all the hopes of the Menagerie faithful. And suddenly she didn't feel so insignificant anymore, or like a mere visitor to this strange world. Responsibility for an entire culture rested on her shoulders because of that scroll. Creatures everywhere were counting on her—on the fulfillment of a promise the Zookeeper had made to them long ago: that he would not abandon them and that he would send someone.

That someone was Mariel Stone. She was the chosen one. She passed a hand over her temples, feeling lightheaded and overwhelmed. Swallowing hard, Mariel squared her shoulders. "Well, let's not stand around here then," she said in a small voice that was not quite her own.

"Indeed no," agreed Simeon, whose attention had wandered to the sky. "Because in every army, there are also spies. And that doesn't look like Marcus up there."

Mariel whirled and stared up into the blue expanse. A distant black speck was quickly multiplying into a cloud of specks. Mariel involuntarily cowered. "Marcus wouldn't happen to have any soot-covered brothers, would he?"

Simeon's strong teeth gripped the back of Mariel's shirt and the huge workhorse hiked her off her feet, tossing her to the side of the path. She landed, stumbling and already running with her companions right behind her, making for a little copse dense with underbrush. Mariel dove for cover and felt sharp brambles tearing at her clothes and skin, but she lay still. The horse and llama did not follow her inside, but instead meandered along the bordering edge of the trees, grazing at a casual pace.

Mariel tried to smother her breathing in dead leaves and damp earth. Blood was beginning to trickle annoyingly from a dozen scratches in her skin, and she squeezed her eyes shut and tried to ignore it, concentrating on her rapid heartbeat instead. The angry screeching of birds was coming closer, and Mariel warily turned her head to one side and risked a glance upwards. An entire flock of crows rushed past, cawing so menacingly that Mariel cringed.

Just as suddenly as they came, the crows were gone, flying over the distant hills and out of sight.

"Steady," whispered Simeon.

It was a full ten minutes before Mariel's companions allowed her to leave the safety of the underbrush. The girl was scowling and ruefully studying a hundred tiny red scratches, most of which had stopped bleeding by now.

Anna nuzzled her arm. "I'm sorry, little one."

"What's so bad about the crows around here?" Mariel wanted to know, picking leaves from her hair as they started off again.

"They're messengers and spies for the Other Side," Simeon replied, twitching an ear in Mariel's direction. "Those probably didn't pose much of a threat to us, fortunately. They were in a hurry."

"Which is troubling news in itself," Anna hastened to add, seeing Mariel's annoyed reaction. "Something must have happened. I don't like how fast they were flying."

"Well, whatever," Mariel mumbled. "But before I leap into brambles again, I'm going to make sure I really need to!"

Simeon chuffed. "If they'd seen us, they'd have reported it. Believe me, those scratches were not gained for nothing."

They plodded steadily on, not speaking much. The

remainder of their journey was untroubled by any creatures who might have borne them ill will, though once Mariel paused to stare a long time into a thicket. She wasn't entirely sure, but she thought, for a moment, that a pair of gleaming yellow eyes had been glaring out at her. Anna and Simeon were both oblivious, yet far more vigilant and alert than Mariel was, so the girl shrugged it off and walked on.

They crested a hill and there, before them, was their destination: a beautiful rainbow city made of some translucent, glasslike material Mariel never imagined existed. It reminded her of the colored marbles that children from Green Valley liked to collect. It was quite large, spanning over the shallow valley for miles in every direction, and the fringes to the east and west were still under construction. It was easy to see why Anna and Simeon didn't even consider going around the rainbow city. The pathway passed right through the heart of it; a detour skirting its edge could take a week.

"Wow," she breathed.

Simeon sighed and shook his head. Anna gave the girl a sidelong glance. "Looks can be deceiving," she warned. "Now listen carefully. We're going in now, and we will meet people you're not going to agree with. Keep your thoughts to yourself until we're safely clear of the place. If we get separated, stay to the path and get out of the city as quickly as possible. Wait for us further down the road, at the clock tower called The Sign of the Times. If we don't arrive within an hour, keep going. It is imperative that you reach the inn before night falls."

"Wait...wait a minute," implored Mariel, her voice quavering a little. "What do you mean by 'separated'? If we're separated, what...what will that mean, exactly?"

"That you're on your own, and you'll have to trust the Zookeeper," said Simeon sternly. He nudged her hard with his muzzle. "Come on. We're wasting time."

Mariel was forced to walk down the hill in front of the workhorse and the llama, still trying to resolve possibilities in her panicking mind. She'd come to trust and depend on Simeon and Anna in a very short amount of time—probably because of the danger she'd faced already, she mused—and the idea of going on without them was a disquieting one.

An archway guarded the entrance to the city. Multicolored neon letters across the top announced: *Rainbow Haven—One step away from heaven.*

Mariel wrinkled her brow. That was a pretty brazen statement, but it definitely piqued her curiosity. Looking at the archway now, up close, she saw a murky reflection of herself and realized that the archway was covered with some kind of liquid-based mirroring substance. Uncertainly, she stopped, staring into the rippling fluid.

"It will feel a bit odd when you pass through it," Anna told her. "But Simeon's right, we haven't got much time. Just remember everything I told you, little one. And no matter what, never leave the road."

With that, the llama stepped through the archway, her head disappearing first through the shimmering gel, and then her shoulders and forelimbs, until finally it enveloped her completely. Mariel gazed after her and swallowed hard.

"Go on. I'm right behind you," encouraged Simeon.

Mariel steeled herself and stuck a tentative finger through the unstable wall. It felt just like jello. After another hesitation and a glance back at the resolute workhorse, Mariel closed her eyes, held her breath, and plunged through to the other side.

It was like entering a smooth bubble. The moment she passed into Rainbow Haven, Mariel felt like a fish out of water. She had trouble breathing the thickly humid air. When she opened her eyes, she stumbled to a halt to stare about her in utter fascination.

The ground was blue—the flagstones in the path, the grass, the rocks, the flowers—all of it. It was all exactly the same shade of electric blue, matching perfectly the sky above them. Gray squirrels bearing tiny buckets of blue paint and little brushes were everywhere, meticulously painting everything on the ground blue and, curiously enough, scurrying backwards as they went.

On either side of the blue avenue, trees were growing, but they were upside down. What must have been the green canopies were buried underground, while the roots made grotesque patterns against the summer sun. Moles, which Mariel had never seen off the ground, populated the tree roots, spreading mats of imitation grass turf across the sky.

Houses were built with flat foundations upwards, so that they balanced precariously on the apex points of their roofs. A large sign greeted the travelers: *Nevah Wobniar—Nevaeh morf yawa pets eno.*

Mariel's jaw fell open. "What on earth…?"

Anna spoke through clamped teeth. "Remember what I told you," she gritted under her breath, watching the busy squirrels.

Mariel nodded absently, but the puzzled furrow in her brow deepened as they moved farther into Nevah Wobniar. Mariel stepped around a squirrel, who was so intent on painting every blade of grass beside the path blue that he never even noticed her.

Mariel risked a question. "What does 'Nevah Wobniar' mean?"

"It's Rainbow Haven backwards," replied Simeon quietly. "No more questions."

As they moved on again and progressed deeper into Nevah Wobniar, they were beginning to encounter the natives. They were almost as much of a shock to Mariel as their natural habitat, if the backwards surroundings could qualify as natural.

Songbirds flew upside down, working doubly hard to flap their wings in that awkward position while their stomachs pointed up to the sky. Mariel couldn't begin to fathom how they could see where they were going. Every other creature—jet-black apes, skinny white cows with long horns, and a lone yellow-and-black-spotted leopard—walked backwards. Mariel saw a gray goat back against the front of a house. He stepped into black rubber hoof covers with suction cups on the bottoms, and easily climbed the outside wall until he reached the front door. He turned completely upside down so he could walk on the floor, then he shut the door after him. Mariel could hear his muffled *thook-thook-thook* as he moved down the hall.

She was stunned, almost speechless. Her companions were no less appalled.

"Marcus wasn't exaggerating," whispered Anna. "Walk like them, little one." So saying, she turned her rump and, with some difficulty, backed down the pathway through Nevah Wobniar. Mariel followed her example and couldn't understand why these creatures persisted in their efforts to adopt a mode of such unnatural locomotion. Mariel promptly tripped on a blue flagstone and landed hard on her rear end.

She got up, muttering under her breath and rubbing the seat of her pants. Simeon couldn't see where he was going; he backed into her and stepped hard on her foot.

"Ow!" hollered Mariel, pulling her offended toes from beneath the crushing hoof. Simeon whirled with an expression of shocked hurt and put his muzzle close to her in a comforting manner.

"I'm terribly sorry…please don't draw attention to us," he hissed softly, his concerned gaze on Mariel's foot, which she suspended above the ground as waves of electrifying pain coursed through it. Several heads had already turned to look at them, and a yellow canary, preoccupied with staring while flying upside down, slammed into a tree and dropped to the ground in a little heap of yellow feathers, unconscious.

"Ow…" Mariel grimaced. "I mean… Ow, baby! I love this backwards stuff," she said, just loud enough for the nearest creatures to hear.

"Hush!" hissed Anna in alarm. "Let's get out of here…"

Anna and Simeon backed down the widening avenue with Mariel stumbling backwards, trying not to hobble. She was slightly relieved to see the onlookers disperse and continue on with their backwards lives. The canary was sitting up, shaking his feathers and twittering dizzily.

The agony in Mariel's foot was growing with each step. They went on, past strange rainbow-colored statues in twisted shapes Mariel couldn't define.

Once they were relatively alone, the llama glanced around for anyone who might be eavesdropping. Then she spoke. "You don't want to engage any of them in conversation. They're mastering the art of talking backwards."

"What?!" Mariel couldn't hide her indignation; her foot still throbbed, and she blamed it entirely on Nevah Wobniar's strange customs. "Sounds like they're mastering the art of utter stupidity."

"Quietly," urged Anna. "I told you things were getting out of hand. We're beyond the town square now. Let's sit down and have a bite to eat."

Anna led them into a makeshift blue alcove, partially sheltered by upside-down trees. They were all glad of the break. Mariel seated herself on a blue log, and Simeon, who felt horrible for causing such a dreadful accident, kicked a medium-sized blue boulder over to Mariel so she could rest her foot. She smiled gratefully at him and set her hand on his cheekbone, and the old gray workhorse froze under her soft touch and let out a deep sigh.

"It's going to be all right," Mariel soothed.

Simeon fixed his dark eyes on her. "What? Your foot, our mission, or life in general?"

"All three, Simeon," replied Mariel with a self-confidence that surprised her.

Anna had been roaming around the area, nosing here and there, and finally she returned with a disgruntled expression on her whiskery muzzle. "For goodness sakes, a creature can't get a bite to eat around here. All that grass is covered in blue paint and it's entirely inedible." She cast a sorrowfully pleading glance at Mariel. "I'm sorry to ask this of you, but may we—?"

"Of course." Mariel wriggled out of her pack, opened it, and took out two small biscuits. She poked a hole in each with her fingers and stuffed them with raisins, then offered the snack to her companions. "Highly nutritious," she explained.

Simeon grinned between mighty chomps, regaining a little of his good humor. "And highly delicious."

Mariel smiled, then fixed her own biscuit with raisins. It was perhaps a strange thing to eat, but raisins provided a lot of energy; she would be able to travel farther on raisins than on most other substances. She fed a second biscuit to each of her friends, then withdrew a piece of dried venison jerky for herself. She hadn't taken more than two bites when she suddenly froze. Yellow eyes glared at her from the trees for a moment, then winked away.

Mariel swallowed hard and slowly sat up straight. "We're being watched," she whispered.

Simeon's ears were flat against his neck. "By more than one wolf," he replied, swiveling his wary gaze from one side to the other. "There are three of them…"

A chill shot down Mariel's spine. She dropped the jerky and pulled her pack close as if for protection, watching the woods. The yellow eyes glimmered again, closer this time, and unmistakably framed by a furry gray ruff belonging to a wolf.

Anna gulped down the last of her biscuit. "Simeon, we have to get her out of here…"

"Put on your pack." Simeon's voice was deadly quiet.

Mariel seized it and slung it over her shoulder just as a black wolf sprang snarling from the trees, his yellow fangs bared and his murderous glare on Mariel. Mariel screamed and ducked as a massive kick from Simeon sent the wolf cowering back. Instantly, two gray wolves broke cover and joined the black one, and, growling, they menaced the three companions. Anna stomped her small hooves and stood protectively in front of a very frightened Mariel, who was picking herself off the ground.

All three wolves crouched, and Simeon and Anna braced themselves. The wolves struck with such force that Mariel let out a cry and stumbled backwards. Simeon took on both grays, and fur flew from the furious tussle. Mariel had never dreamed a horse could roar like Simeon did. One wolf landed on his neck, biting viciously, but the huge workhorse shook him off and stomped on him. There was a horrible crunch, and the wolf lay still. Mariel whimpered and looked away from the awful sight of mangled fur and blood.

While Simeon scuffled with the remaining gray wolf, Anna was having trouble battling the black. She pummeled him with her little hooves, but it didn't phase him as he leaped tirelessly again and again for her vulnerable throat. Anna's dark eyes were rolling in fear as she defended herself, doggedly refusing to let him pass and get to Mariel. But he was wearing down her strength. Mariel looked around frantically, then snatched a blue rock and threw it at the wolf. It landed a stunning blow across his sensitive muzzle, and blood flowed from the gash.

The black wolf turned on the girl, growling. He licked blood from his fangs and glared. "You shouldn't have done that, missy."

Before Mariel could answer, Anna leaped forward and thrashed his ribs, sending him rolling to the ground. He scrambled to his paws and rushed Anna's delicate llama limbs. Anna went down with a scream.

"Run, Mariel! Run!"

Blind with terror, Mariel whirled and plunged away on rubbery legs. The bouncing pack slid off her shoulder, but Mariel didn't stop to retrieve it. The last thing she saw was the black wolf closing his jaws around the struggling llama's furry neck. Mariel screamed as she tripped and went skidding down a muddy slope into the forest below.

CHAPTER
NINE

A wild flight through the upside-down forest found Mariel somewhere in the midst of trees—lost, breathless, packless, scratched and sore-hearted. Shadows seemed to chase her; leering wolves darted behind the trees and vanished, only to reappear somewhere else, or so it seemed to Mariel's overwrought imagination. Mariel ran until she could go no further. Whirling in terror, she faced the trees behind her, expecting to be finished at any moment. There was nothing. But her legs wouldn't hold her up anymore. She fell to her knees as tears overwhelmed her, and she buried her face in the damp earth.

"Anna," she whispered brokenly. "Simeon, Anna…"

Harsh laughter interrupted her misery, and Mariel shot upright, her frightened eyes searching the tree root canopy for the unwelcome interloper. But whoever or whatever was laughing at her remained invisible.

"Ah-ah-ah-ah-ah!"

Wiping fiercely at her tear-smudged cheeks, Mariel stood up and glowered. "Show yourself," she muttered without spirit.

A frowsy-headed white bird with dark gray-blue wings popped out from behind a tree trunk. "Don't you know kookaburras laugh, missy?"

"Er…lots of birds laugh," answered Mariel in a deadpan tone.

The kookaburra puffed out his little white chest. "Ah-ah-ah! Not like kookaburras. Kookaburras are the champs at laughing. And *I'm* the champ at laughing backwards."

Mariel eyed the brazen bird, not at all in the mood to deal with his attitude. "Yes, I see that. But I notice you're not *talking* backwards."

The kookaburra glared accusingly at her. "You started it," he blustered, fluffing his feathers. "I really can talk backwards. See wanna?"

"Oh, no, please don't." Mariel regretted bringing it up. She sighed and turned her back on him, staring dully around her at the mass of upside-down trees. They all looked the same, and she had no idea where she was. She glanced sidelong at the kookaburra. "Could you point me in the direction of the road?"

"Way that," returned the bird with a smirk on his beak, pointing towards the setting sun.

81

"Thank you." Mariel didn't look up at him and she refused to bend to the rules—the same stupid rules that were responsible for the deaths of her friends. How she was going to accomplish her mission now, she didn't know, and right then she didn't care. The fresh memory of the wolf attack kept replaying in her mind, and she couldn't think of anything else. It made her heartsick, knowing that it had all been her fault. If Mariel weren't there on this ridiculous mission, Anna and Simeon would still be back at the barn, living their quiet lives and waiting for their Chosen One.

Mariel shook her head and started off westwards through the forest. The Zookeeper made a lousy choice; that's all there was to it. He ought to have sent Gabe. Gabe would have done better than throwing a rock at a wolf's muzzle. Gabe could have saved them...

A lump rose in Mariel's throat and her thoughts melted into numb oblivion.

The kookaburra fluttered his wing after her. "Bye good! Long so! Well thee fare!" He paused and crossed his eyes, thinking hard. Then he counted off his feathers one at a time and recited carefully, "Place happy a to you lead path your may!"

Mariel bit her tongue, too angry to snap at him, and walked on without looking back as he broke into another long peal of backwards laughter. As soon as she could find that blue road, she vowed to leave Nevah Wobniar and this Menagerie altogether. She'd return the Zookeeper's scroll and go home. It was pointless for her to keep going when she obviously wasn't cut out to fill such a crucial role. She could make speeches and stand up for what she believed in, but there was a world of difference between that and taking responsibility for the salvation of an entire society.

In the midst of Mariel's brooding, a very strange conversation interrupted her thoughts from above.

"I'm telling you, the twig goes on the *outside*."

"It does not!"

Mariel shook her head, then looked up to find two black starlings bickering in the midst of building an upside-down nest. Judging from their deep voices, they were both males. Mariel guessed they were too involved in their discussion to revert to backwards language.

"It's a *support* twig, you dingbat. The females always put these on the outside."

"No, it goes like this! Watch."

There was some rustling about, and suddenly the nest plummeted from the tree branches and landed in a heap at Mariel's feet. Mariel stopped abruptly and stared at it, then squinted up at the birds. They were both disgruntled, and they completely ignored the girl. One slapped its wing into the back of the other's head.

"I told you."

"Hey, gimme a break. It's hard building a nest upside down."

The first starling aimed his wing at the nest. "Now, what should we do, hmm? Raise our chicks in a grounded nest? The wolves will have us for breakfast."

"Oh, hey, that reminds me of one little dilemma I thought of," chirped the second bird, heedless of his companion's sarcasm. He rubbed his feathers over the back of his sore head. "How are we gonna find an egg to raise?"

Mariel's jaw fell open.

"Who cares?" muttered his grouchy companion, puffing his feathers with a dismal sigh.

"I care," argued the other, who seemed younger—or perhaps less dominant. "If we have no egg, then there's no chick, and we can't have a family."

The first starling glared. "Jeez, you think?"

He nodded vigorously. "Uh-huh. Maybe we should ask one of the females if—"

"Who needs stinking females?" exploded the first bird furiously. Mariel blanched at the hatred directed towards avian members of her own gender.

"We do," began the other diminutively, "if we want chicks."

"I'd sooner incubate a rock until it hatches," interrupted the cranky starling. "I'm not asking a female for anything."

Mariel shuddered. She walked carefully around the fallen nest and continued through the woods, quickening her pace to put some distance between her and the creepy little birds.

"You know, *I* could ask her," offered the younger bird.

There was the sound of a sharp smack. "Birdbrain! I've got better ideas."

"Like what?"

There was a pause. "I don't know yet, I'm thinkin'."

"Are you gonna lay an egg yourself?"

Mariel hurried out of earshot, feeling sick to her stomach. She'd had quite enough of that talk. *No wonder they didn't bother reversing their sentences*, Mariel thought wryly. *They don't need to. Their normal speech is backwards already.*

Blessed silence enveloped her again as she wandered deeper into unknown territory. She was still afraid of being followed, and she glanced over her shoulder at every few steps. Why didn't they come? Because they were satisfied with their day's kill? A horrible vision of the wolves hauling off the horse and llama carcasses to their lair crossed Mariel's mind, and she let out a little whimpering cry of pain and shoved her thoughts away. She cried as she walked, and she had to keep a thick darkness from clouding her mind. Narrowing her eyes, she focused on following the westward sun, but her feet wandered—like her disoriented thoughts.

After what seemed like hours, Mariel knew she was lost. Nothing looked familiar, yet it all did: trees, upside down, spreading a web of roots against the afternoon sky. Mariel had a sinking feeling that she was going the wrong way, a notion that was suddenly confirmed when she reached a bluff at the edge of the forest.

Mariel stood on the outcropping and gazed over an incredible world. A dazzling rainbow city, bursting with activity from animals who were all walking and working backwards. Huts that resembled upside-down gumdrops dotted the clearing far below her perch. The ground was bright blue, of course, and huge mats of artificial grass were being built across the sky, casting a shadow over part of the city. The whole air sparkled with rainbows from tiny prisms that were embedded in the hut walls and scattered across the grounds, hanging from the roots of upside-down bushes.

Mariel stood there, gazing down for a long time. Animal couples strolled paw-in-paw along the blue cobblestones, and much to the girl's chagrin, she realized they were either in pairs of two males or two females.

"This is so far from Noah's Ark," Mariel muttered, shaking her head.

Behind her, someone—or something—cleared its throat. Mariel almost leaped out of her skin and nearly took a plunge off the bluff into the rainbow city below. Whirling, she found a grinning hedgehog, standing upright and clasping a small blue flower between his paws.

"You to day good," he greeted her.

Recovering from her fright, Mariel stepped away from the edge and sighed. "Please don't talk backwards to me."

The hedgehog cocked his head, puzzled, and blinked large black eyes at her. "Why not? Everyone talks backwards here."

"Not me," answered Mariel dryly. "I'm not from here. I'm just passing through."

Chuckling in a little voice, the hedgehog trundled towards her and gave a long, drawn-out "Ooooh." His back was covered in little white-tipped black spines—a contrast to his soft-furred stomach—and he had what Mariel decided was an absolutely adorable face. "That explains a lot," he said, holding up his flower. "Here. I just dug this up today. I'm Ben, and welcome to…to Rainbow Haven."

"Thank you, kindly," responded Mariel, accepting the little blue forget-me-not. She tucked it behind her ear. "Is it really Rainbow Haven, or Nevah Wobniar?"

The hedgehog's countenance fell, and he sidled closer to her, lowering his voice. "Well…it used to be Rainbow Haven. But it's not anymore," he told her sadly.

Mariel looked at the city below her, then back at Ben. "I really want to leave this place and go home," she said plaintively.

Ben beckoned to her with his tiny paw. "Me, too. But we can't yet."

Mariel latched onto his words. "Who's 'we'?"

"Come home with me, and I'll show you." Ben beamed up at her.

The invitation made Mariel immediately nervous. Ben didn't seem threatening so far, but Nevah Wobniar had taught her to suspect even the most harmless-appearing of creatures. Frowning, Mariel cautiously nodded. "For…for just a little while, maybe. I have to find the road and be out of here before nightfall."

Gripping Mariel's pant leg, Ben trundled off through the upside-down woods. "Were you looking for the road, missie?"

"Yes. And it's Mariel."

"Ah, Mariel, you were going the wrong way."

"I gathered."

"Didn't you ask someone for directions?"

"A kookaburra, who…" Mariel broke off with a gasp. "Who was talking backwards." She blinked, and sudden wrath stirred inside her. "The road is due east, isn't it?"

The hedgehog patted her calf. "Ah, don't be so hard on yourself. I'm not used to it, either, and I've lived here all my life. But here we are. This is my place." He pointed to an inconspicuous hole in the ground.

Mariel stopped. "Um, Ben? Little problem here…"

"Hm? Oh." He waved his paw at her dismissively. "You can't fit in my house, but that's okay. Wait here." He disappeared down the hole. A moment later, Mariel heard his little voice echoing in the hollow space. "Everybody up! We have a visitor!"

There was some shuffling about and soft speech Mariel couldn't understand, followed by little exclamations of surprise. Within seconds, Ben popped out of the hole, followed closely by another hedgehog who looked like him, but with softer eyes. Four tiny hoglets came after them, looking like spiny furballs.

Ben presented them with a flourish. "Allow me to introduce my lovely wife, Marcy, and these are our three boys: Davy, Gary, and Joey. And this is our little sunshine, Jordyce."

Blushing, Jordyce hid slightly behind her mother's spines. "I'm a girl," she told Mariel bashfully.

Mariel crouched down to be closer to their level. "I promise not to mix you up with your brothers."

Jordyce blushed and all but disappeared behind Marcy.

Joey sneezed. Marcy waved shyly to Mariel. "He has a bit of a cold just now," she explained. She smiled at the girl. "Dear, would you like some tea?"

Mariel smiled, charmed. "Thank you, I would."

Marcy vanished down the hole. Left out in the open, Jordyce watched Mariel with wary curiosity in her bright black eyes. The hoglet boys grew restless and started scuffling about. Mariel sank gratefully onto a fallen log while Ben sat down before her and made himself comfortable.

"Lovely family you have," Mariel remarked quietly, watching them roll in the mud and run around with childish abandon.

Ben smiled. "Ah, thank you. I think so too, if I may say so." He sighed. "I wish I could move them all away from this place."

"Why don't you?" Mariel wondered, gazing at him.

"I can't." Ben held out his small paws. "Where would we go? Every city in the Menagerie is becoming corrupt in various ways. Here, at least, we've not been bothered. We live away from the heart of Rainbow Haven, and few creatures disturb our peace. Besides that, moving takes money, and we aren't...I mean, we're sort of...well, we're poor." His spiny shoulders drooped at that sad fact. "We're trying to make it, but I'm just a flower-digger."

"You...you dig up flowers for a living?" guessed Mariel.

Ben nodded. "Mm-hm. That's one thing this culture has done—no flowers grow anymore, 'cept underground, and someone has to dig them up. It's harder than it looks, too. And it doesn't pay very much."

"Oh," said Mariel softly, her fingers going to her ear to touch the flower he'd given her earlier. She understood now what the gift of a forget-me-not was worth. Part of her wanted to give it back, but these folks were generous, and Mariel knew such a suggestion would upset them.

"But look on the bright side," Ben declared abruptly, shaking himself from his troubles. "At least the ground here isn't blue, eh?"

Mariel laughed, and Ben chuckled with her. Marcy emerged from the hole with a tiny teacup of yellowish-brown liquid and an equally tiny saucer with four or five shredded dandelion leaves on it. Jordyce immediately huddled behind her mother and peeked out at Mariel.

"Here you are, dear," said Marcy with maternal warmth, setting the dwarfed items in Mariel's outstretched palm. "Would you like some sugar?"

"Oh, no, thank you." Mariel smiled at the kindly hedgehog. Holding the little cup gingerly between thumb and forefinger, she took a sip, and the tea was gone before Mariel could taste it. "Delicious," she remarked.

Marcy glowed with pleasure. "It's just dandelion root tea," she explained. Her black eyes darted to two of her boys, still wrestling in the mud. "Davy! Joey! For heaven's sakes, come here! You'll both have a bath this afternoon."

Groaning, Davy pulled his brother from the oozing mud, and they waddled up to their mother. Jordyce backed away to avoid getting her spines muddy. Joey sneezed. Mariel felt something on her shoe and looked down to find Gary climbing her pant leg, getting mud all over her jeans. He perched on her knee and grinned up at her, grubby and content.

"Hey, I's wondering…you gonna eat all that?" He pointed at the saucer of dandelion leaves.

Marcy was horrified. "Why, Gary!" Her creamy cheeks turned pink, and she looked apologetically at Mariel. "He just had lunch a little while ago."

"I know," protested the little hedgehog, his appealing black eyes blinking up at Mariel. "But I's always hungry."

Mariel laughed good-naturedly and addressed Gary. "You like dandelions that much?"

Gary bounced. "I loves 'um," he told her.

Mariel leaned close as if confiding in him. "I've never had one before."

Gary's beady eyes widened. "You hasn't?"

"Nope. And I'm a bit nervous to try them. So you eat one first and tell me what it's like, and if you think it's all right, I'll eat one. Deal?"

"Deal! Deal!" Gary quivered with excitement and grasped a sliver of dandelion leaf carefully between his paws, cramming it into his mouth all at once. He spoke with rounded cheeks. "I's yummy!"

"Really?" Mariel gave him an exaggeratedly doubtful expression. "All right, but I'm really going out on a limb here. You're absolutely certain they're good?"

"Oh, yeth!" exalted the little hedgehog with his mouth full, bouncing on her knee. "Twy it, twy it!"

Mariel made a big show of shutting her eyes tightly and biting off a tiny piece of dandelion, trying not to think of Ortho and other weedkillers back home. She'd never look at a dandelion the same way again. Gary was right, too: dandelions had a gentle flavor, and Mariel decided they were better than lettuce.

She opened one eye. "Not bad," she assented.

"Yippee!" celebrated Gary, whirling in a circle and nearly tumbling to the ground. Mariel's hand flew out and caught him in the nick of time, his little spines rough against her palm, but Gary never noticed. He was in ecstasy. "Eat 'nuther one!"

Ben and Marcy were laughing in sheepish embarrassment at their little one's antics. Even Jordyce was smiling. Davy sat quietly beside his mother, and Mariel noticed the hungry look in his dark eyes, so she asked him to sample the next sprig before she trusted another bite. Between sneezes, Joey also tested Mariel's dandelions very carefully, and Jordyce nibbled daintily at the pieces Mariel gave her. In no time at all, the saucer was clean. Mariel decided she'd never had a more enjoyable supper in her life.

"So what brings you to Rainbow Haven, Mariel?" Ben asked.

Mariel shifted uncomfortably, and her free hand strayed to her jeans' pocket which carried the Zookeeper's tiny scroll. She didn't want to reveal the whole purpose of her mission. While the young hedgehogs munched, Mariel told how she'd been chased through the forest by wolves.

At the mention of the dreadful predators, all four hoglets gasped and rolled into prickly balls. Mariel clapped a hand over her mouth. "I'm sorry! I didn't mean to scare them…"

Marcy hugged Joey, who uncurled slightly to sneeze before huddling against his mother again. "It's all right," she soothed her baby, but she was talking to Mariel. Jordyce unrolled herself, dashed behind Marcy, and curled up again.

Gary's head poked out from between his spines. "I's not skeered," he informed her boldly. "I just likes to do that, fer fun."

Not to be outdone by his younger brother's bravado, Davy emerged also. "Me, too. So how'd you get away?"

"I don't know," replied Mariel, her face falling. She hadn't the heart to tell them about her companions.

Marcy cleared her throat and exchanged glances with her husband, then looked up at the girl. "Are you still hungry?"

"Me? No!" Mariel couldn't help laughing at Gary, who was busily picking leaves out of his teeth. She smiled at the hedgehog wife. "That was wonderful, Marcy. Thank you."

Marcy flushed, then clapped her paws twice. "Okay, kids, bath-time!"

A chorus of moans erupted from the three boys, but Jordyce's dark eyes lit up. Gary grinned at Mariel. "Bye!" He slid down her leg, landing neatly beside her shoe. Mariel waved after them, and the hedgehogs waddled off with Joey last in line, sneezing.

Mariel shook her head and smiled at Ben when they were alone. "What a cute family, Ben."

Ben chuckled. "Yeah, I'll keep them." After Mariel's laughter subsided, he was all business. "I'd offer to let you stay with us, but I can't, for obvious reasons." He gestured to their little hole, which wasn't nearly large enough to accommodate anyone of Mariel's size. Then he pointed up to the sky, which Mariel saw was orange with sunset. "You're too far north to go back the way you came. You can't leave Rainbow Haven before nightfall, I'm afraid. The only thing you can do is head east, where you'll find the road, and exit Rainbow Haven. From there, you'll find a clock tower called The Sign of the Times. You can rest there tonight and come back through Rainbow Haven in the morning."

Mariel's heart plummeted at the thought of staying where she'd planned to rendezvous with Anna and Simeon before tragedy struck. Pursing her lips, she nodded gravely to Ben and offered him her forefinger. "Thank you for everything," she said quietly, and she meant it. It was good to forget her troubles for a little while.

Ben touched her finger with his paw. "May the Master watch over you."

"You too, Ben."

Mariel set off through the darkening wood. Shafts of departing sunlight played through the upside down trees, then disappeared altogether. Bats left their roosts in the gathering twilight, and Mariel quickened her pace as they flapped overhead.

It was dark by the time her feet struck the path. Mariel sighed in relief, and she might've kissed the stones if they weren't covered in chemical-scented blue paint. Wearily, she followed the road by the light of the half-moon, and, as Ben had said, it was only a short journey to the north gate.

Mariel's heart ached as she stepped beyond the bubble-like substance and into the normal world. It was getting colder, and she shivered. Not far away, she saw the clock tower rising against the starry sky, its white clock face showing 8:20, and Mariel stifled a yawn. She was exhausted. The thought of a warm bed and a pillow gave her strength for the last few steps before she reached the tower.

Mariel stopped and stared. Suddenly she broke into a run. Beside the clock tower stood the silhouettes of a llama and a workhorse, and the workhorse held between his teeth something large and bulky: a pack.

CHAPTER
TEN

Mariel threw herself to the ground and sobbed blindly on Simeon's thickly feathered hoof for a long time. The warm, solid feel of his leg convinced her that he was real, and she clung to him, afraid to let go, as if he would vanish the moment she did. Simeon and Anna nuzzled the girl's quivering back.

"I thought you were…" Mariel couldn't bear to finish her sentence. She hugged Simeon's huge hoof, her tears matting the coarse white hairs against the workhorse's pastern.

"Hush, dear," whispered Anna, her voice strangely hoarse. "It's cold out here, and you'll catch a chill. Simeon, let's get her inside…" Mariel was almost too weak to move. She felt her companions nuzzling her ribs, and she draped an arm over each strong neck as they pulled her to her feet and helped her stumble inside the clock tower.

It wasn't really a clock tower at all. The Sign of the Times was an old-fashioned but well-kept inn. Animals sat or stood at tables, eating and chattering, while a roaring fire blazed in the hearth at one end of the room. The bar was split in two, and Mariel noticed through blurry vision that one side of it wasn't a counter at all, but a long communal trough, where various four-legged creatures were drinking—an enormous hippopotamus, two or three baby elephants, and a red fox. The main bar counter's stools were occupied by bearded old men debating dry subjects in long, drawn-out speeches. They looked, Mariel thought, as if they'd been sitting there for hundreds of years, endlessly engaged in pointless conversation.

Once they were illuminated by yellow firelight, Mariel noticed Anna was covered in white bandages. One was wrapped around her throat, and others were bound along her fragile legs, and she hobbled slightly as she walked. But her dark eyes were bright, and she held her head high, as if her spirits were unvanquished.

Simeon's attention was on the tall man behind the counter, who had thick gray hair and a white apron tied around his middle. The man seemed to know the old horse. He abruptly left the customers he was serving and beamed a smile at his newest visitors.

"Ah, Simeon! Fair winds blow through my door today."

Simeon pricked his ears. "Good to see you too, Chuck. Is the sitting room available?"

Chuck smiled and rocked back on his heels importantly, tucking his thumbs in the waist of his apron. "For you, Simeon, I always have a place prepared. Go right in. I'll have Leann bring around some pie shortly."

They made their way through the tavern, garnering a variety of stares from its patrons—ranging from the obnoxiously curious to narrowed-eyed suspicion. Mariel thought for sure she was hallucinating because one of the baby elephants at the bar trough didn't look right. Its trunk hung limply and dragged on the ground, and its face was a little longer than rounded baby elephant faces should have been, while its tail was thicker with more than coarse elephant hair, and a little chalky—as if it were painted gray. Narrowing her eyes, Mariel focused on him. At the same moment, the elephant turned its head and met her gaze. Mariel gasped softly and looked quickly away.

She allowed herself to be half-carried into an adjoining sitting room and seated in a comfortable chair before a cozy fire. Mariel struggled to sit up, her pleading eyes on Simeon.

"There was...out there..."

Mercifully Simeon interrupted her. "I saw."

"Spies?"

"This time, no. They're called 'Masqueraders.' It's mostly the donkeys and elephants trying to pass themselves off as the other race. It has everything to do with the arena games and the new government they're setting up here in the Menagerie, in lieu of the Zookeeper. Long story."

"Are...they a threat?" persisted Mariel.

"To us? No."

All the tension drained out of Mariel. She was exhausted.

Once the warmth of the flames hit her, she began to shiver until her teeth chattered. Simeon stayed close to her chair like a strong barrier of protection against the forces of evil. Anna trotted off, and returned soon after with a blanket in her mouth, which she draped over the shaking girl. It was gloriously soft, and Mariel snuggled into it.

"There," the llama said soothingly, rubbing her cotton-soft muzzle against Mariel's cheek.

Mariel gave a little moan and closed her eyes, a feeling of real safety settling over her like the warm blanket. Within moments, she was fast asleep in front of the crackling fire.

The delicious aroma of cooked turkey and bread drifted into Mariel's dreams, drawing her back into the waking world. Looking around through half-lowered eyelids, Mariel found steam rising from a pie on the table, and Anna and Simeon standing close together not far from it, speaking in hushed tones. Simeon nodded in agreement with something Anna said, and glanced at the girl, then did a double take when he saw her struggling to sit up.

"She's alive!" he said, trotting over to her with a broad smile.

"Barely," Mariel mumbled. "What time is it?"

"Pretty late," answered Anna, remaining near the table. "We were wondering if we should wake you for supper or let you sleep through until morning."

Mariel shrugged noncommittally. "It didn't matter, really. But I *am* hungry."

Simeon's head came around, his ears cocked at odd angles, and he studied her carefully as she rose and took a seat at the table. She pulled the turkey pie close and gazed down on it without much interest, then picked up a fork and reluctantly dug into it. It was warm and hearty, but the delicious fare did nothing to raise her spirits.

"What's with the long face?" Simeon wanted to know.

Mariel stopped in mid-chew and looked at him in surprise. "*You* have a long face, Simeon."

"A compliment, I hope."

"It is." Mariel took another bite and was quick to change the subject. "Aren't you guys going to have some?"

Horse and llama exchanged glances. "We're herbivores, dear."

Mariel raised her eyebrows, then eyed her turkey pie and looked embarrassed. "Ah, sorry. I forgot." She ate in uncomfortable silence, feeling Simeon watching her and knowing she hadn't thrown him off-track. If anything, she'd proven his hunch that something was the matter.

Her fork hit the bowl with a metallic clang. "I can't do this, guys."

Anna took a step closer and frowned at the pie. "What's wrong with it?"

"Oh, no, it's not the pie." Mariel sighed. "I know you both have a lot of hopes riding on me, but I'm not the one to save the Menagerie."

"No one's asking you to, little one," answered Anna gently. "That's the Zookeeper's job."

"Yes, but He chose me to pave the way, and I can't do it."

Simeon snorted. "And the wolf attack was paramount to this revelation?"

Mariel stared at her pie as it slowly grew colder. "Among other things."

"You aren't afraid of failure, are you?" persisted the llama.

Mariel gave a dismal nod.

Anna nudged her muzzle firmly against Mariel's shoulder. "The outcome is not your concern." Mariel gave her a sharp glance, but Anna went on. "Failure or success is the Zookeeper's concern. The only thing you have to do is be obedient, and follow the path He told you to take, to whatever end."

"But what if I do fail? What will happen to the Menagerie?" Mariel insisted.

"Who knows? Maybe the Zookeeper is only asking us to follow this path because He has some other goal in mind—one we cannot see yet."

"But there are creatures here who are counting on me."

"No, we're counting on the Zookeeper," Anna replied. "Big difference."

Mariel sighed and stared at her pie, somewhat downcast. "So much could go wrong, though."

"Or right," chuffed Simeon.

Mariel blinked back tears. "But…but I don't want…anything else to happen to you. E- even if it's the Zookeeper's prerogative, or whatever."

The room fell silent. Anna gently nuzzled the girl's cheek. Whirling suddenly, Mariel threw her arms around the llama's fluffy neck and wept bitter tears into her thick fur.

"You could have died," the poor girl whimpered miserably.

At that moment, there came a soft knock on the door.

Mariel sat up, keeping her face close to the llama, sniffing and wiping her eyes. Simeon plodded over to the door and pulled with his teeth at a knotted rope, which Mariel hadn't noticed before and now found peculiar. The door came open, and Mariel realized the rope functioned as a sort of doorknob for beasts who lacked opposable thumbs.

A pretty young girl in a green dress entered the room, bearing a large bowl that seemed a little heavy for her. She shook her long ash-blonde hair out of her face and beamed a bright smile at the room's occupants as she deposited her burden on the table. "The missus thought you might like some of her spinach and cheese casserole," she said politely.

"Oh, Lexi, that's very kind of you!" Anna exclaimed, smiling at her, but hovering near Mariel. "Please give her our sincerest thanks."

Lexi nodded absently, but her wide eyes were on Mariel. She took a tentative step in Mariel's direction. "Are...are you the Chosen One?"

Mariel looked up at her. The title didn't fit. It was far too grand for Mariel Stone from backwards little Green Valley, who was stumbling through an unknown country in some wild attempt to...replace a false scroll with the real one and let in the Zookeeper, who seemed more like an ancient gardener than someone who could rule the Menagerie and set it all in perfect order. Reluctantly, Mariel nodded.

Lexi's young face lit up. "Oh, miss, I'm so glad!" she gushed, taking her green skirt between her hands and bobbing a childish curtsy. "We've waited ever so long and—my, what a pretty flower in your hair!" Mariel had forgotten all about the forget-me-not, which was still tucked behind her ear. She drew it out now and looked at it.

Lexi went on, as if she'd never mentioned it. "So you'll be leaving in the morning, right? Well, I don't think those nasty wolves will be coming back, no siree. Simeon scared 'em off good."

"You did?" Mariel gazed at the workhorse in some surprise. Suddenly, she wanted to know the whole story. "How?"

Lexi hugged the great horse's neck, her eyes closed in complete trust. Simeon chuckled and nuzzled her fondly. "I killed one of them and fought off the other two. And now, little one, it's time for bed." He gave her a warm kiss on top of her blonde head and nudged her with his nose.

Lexi skipped to the door, then paused with her hand on the rope. She waved her fingers at Mariel. "Bye!" The door swung shut, and her light footsteps hurried away.

Mariel was still gazing into the heart of the little blue flower. "Was there more to it than that, Simeon?" Simeon snorted and trotted back towards the fire.

"Possibly. I can't say for sure. But I didn't defeat those wolves alone."

"They're still out there, of course." Mariel's voice was deadpan, and she sat perfectly still.

Anna threw a worried glance at Simeon. "Among others, yes."

Mariel shuddered. "Does it hurt to get bitten?" she inquired of Anna.

The llama chuckled dryly. "Quite a bit."

"They're angry, I think." Mariel drew a deep sigh. "Because we—I—got away."

"And we killed a member of their pack," Anna pointed out.

"They want to kill me."

Simeon stood still, gazing into the fire and saying nothing. Anna shrugged her llama shoulders. "If they can, yes."

Twirling the flower between her fingers, Mariel brooded. "Well, I'm not going to let a bunch of mangy wolves stop me."

Anna looked shocked. Simeon's head came around. "Did you say what I just thought you said?"

"Depends on what you thought I said," returned Mariel evenly, watching the flower petals spin. "If you thought I said I wasn't afraid, then no. If you thought I said we aren't going to fail, or possibly die in the attempt, then no. If you thought I said that tomorrow morning, I'm going to continue on this path I set out to follow, then yes."

The next morning, other guests staying at the Sign of the Times complained to Chuck of being awakened in the middle of the night by what sounded like a cheer, coming from the sitting room downstairs, and they wanted to know who was up having a party on the first floor. By that time, Simeon, Mariel and Anna were gone.

CHAPTER
ELEVEN

The morning sun found the trio walking on the path of gold, which grew wider and showed still greater signs of repair the deeper they ventured into the Menagerie. Blue skies and birdsong in the sporadic sycamores cheered them as they trotted on in companionable silence. When they stopped for lunch, Mariel found something even more heartening. Leann, the wife of the innkeeper, Chuck, had replenished their pack with all manner of good things: cinnamon rolls, a generous wedge of white cheese, ham sandwiches, and even sugar cookies. Mariel could hardly believe her eyes.

"Those people, back at the Sign of the Times, were really nice," she remarked, sampling one of the sandwiches. That morning's journey had already given her a healthy appetite.

From where she was grazing beside Simeon, Anna raised her head. "You can always tell who serves the Master and who doesn't," she replied, swallowing a mouthful of grass. "They are coming under increasing suspicion because of that."

Mariel stopped mid-bite and stared. "Did our presence there put them in any danger?"

"Not more than they were in already," Anna hastened to assure her.

Mariel wasn't satisfied, and the sandwiches suddenly tasted like cardboard. An image of Chuck and Leann's little girl Lexi drifted across her mind, followed by a menacing ring of wolves surrounding the inn. Mariel shuddered and stuffed the remainder of her lunch in her pack, then hefted it to her shoulder.

"Let's go," she muttered resolutely, rising to her feet. Anna and Simeon glanced at each other, then set off behind her.

A whole line of lemmings moseyed along the golden road, following each other exactly, so that when they twisted and turned, they looked to Mariel like a comical caterpillar. A fat mother quail, who reminded Mariel of Mrs. Shoemaker back home in Green Valley, waddled along with nine chicks trailing in her wake. The one at the end of the line was causing trouble with the sister just ahead of him, bringing a wistful smile to Mariel's lips as she thought of mischievous Bobby Shoemaker. He, along with everyone and everything familiar, seemed so very far away.

A long-eared hare was sleeping fitfully beside the path, kicking his large hind foot at something in a dream, and

Mariel almost didn't see the tortoise until she heard him chuckling at the unconscious hare. Mariel barely avoided stepping on him at the last second and hopped sideways, her sole just skimming the top of his shell. Unfazed, the tortoise inched along on his laborious journey.

Traffic on the roadway was greater at this hour, Mariel realized as they passed a magnificent lion. Sunlight caught in his glorious mane, rippling and glittering like a gold ocean. His eyes, when they met Mariel's, were deep with understanding and kindness. Remarkably, Mariel wasn't afraid of him.

Then they encountered a brunette girl, about Mariel's age, wearing a blue-checked dress and curious red slippers. A black wire-haired terrier poked his head from her picnic basket and was carrying on an energetic conversation with her.

"I tell you, this doesn't look familiar to me at all," the little dog barked.

The girl laughed. "You were asleep in the basket for most of the trip, Otto."

The dog disappeared under the flap, and the basket bumped and jolted in agitation. Suddenly his frowsy head reappeared. "I still think we took a wrong turn back there! Never ask a raven for directions."

"I'm sorry you don't like ravens all that much, Otto," said the girl, shaking her head in amusement, "but I wasn't about to ask the monkeys for advice. Those monkeys are up to some dreadful mischief, though I'm not sure what yet."

"How do you know?" pressed Otto.

The girl directed a polite nod at Mariel's company as they passed each other. "Because," she patiently answered the persistent terrier, "for one thing, they're acting like they *aren't*. But they go around wearing those funny hats and…and *hooting*, except when someone comes near. Then they look around, whistling and acting like they were doing nothing."

"What does that prove?" blustered Otto.

The girl sighed. "Never you mind. Go back to sleep, and I'll wake you up when we get home."

"*If* we ever get there," muttered the unhappy dog, but he must have obeyed the girl, because there was blessed silence as the two walked away.

That prompted Mariel to pull out her map and study it. There was a fork in the road, according to the diagram. Glancing up, Mariel found the real-life representation immediately in front of them.

"We have to go right, it looks like," she told her companions.

Simeon chuckled. "That seems like the fastest path on the map, but we should take a left turn. These days, it's the quickest way to the Capital. That map's a little outdated."

Mariel grinned at him. "What would I do without my own personal GPS locator system?" she muttered wryly.

Anna looked hopelessly puzzled. "What?"

Mariel burst into laughter. "Never mind. Left route it is. Anything else you'd care to tell me about before we get to wherever we're going? Sightseeing tips? Tourist attractions? Points of historical interest?"

Playfully, Anna nipped at Mariel's loose sleeve, and squealing the girl pulled away and dashed around Simeon. Butterflies caught up with Anna as she gave chase, darting back and forth around the great workhorse, who plodded steadily onward with little concern, as if he were the elected babysitter of two rambunctious children.

Giggling like a schoolgirl at recess, Mariel dashed and raced around Simeon, trying to hide from Anna and sneak up on her at the same time. The llama was surprisingly good at this game. Anna was also laughing like a youngster as she danced back and forth with impossible agility.

Mariel took desperate measures. The girl suddenly ducked

under Simeon's belly and tagged Anna before the llama even saw her. Anna whirled, laughing uncontrollably. "Cheater!" She chased Mariel back to her own side of Simeon, pretending to bite Mariel's calves and catching the denim of Mariel's jeans in her teeth instead. Simeon placidly endured their crazy antics with drooping ears, a little grin twitching the corners of his muzzle. Abruptly he raised his head and grew more attentive.

"All right, kids, that's enough. We've arrived."

Mariel and Anna stopped and stared at the black wrought-iron arch. Something about it reminded Mariel of prison bars. Beyond it, the forest grew dense and let in very little sunlight. A sign at the top of the arch read: *Welcome to the Avian Jungle*. A smaller sign beneath was painted in seeming haste: *Speaking the word "Gravitas" prohibited*.

"Gravitas?" Mariel repeated. "What's wrong with 'gravitas'? What does that word mean?"

"A serious and solemn demeanor," replied Simeon, his forehead slightly furrowed. "Basically the opposite of the way you and Anna were behaving just now."

"I see." The absurdity of the rule brought an incredulous grin to Mariel's features. "And why is that word off-limits, exactly?"

Anna flicked an ear. "I haven't the foggiest idea. But let's refrain from saying gravitas until we're safely out of here, shall we?"

"I'll do my best," sighed Mariel with feigned solemnity. The strangeness of the request still bothered her.

They passed through the arch together, leaving blithe playfulness outside the Avian Jungle. There was no drastic change like there had been in Nevah Wobniar—besides the abrupt loss of light that made it seem as if they'd just entered a rainy day—and that in itself was strange to Mariel. Being prepared for something and finding nothing instead had that effect on her.

A creeping feeling rippled down her spine. She sensed that the trees themselves were watching her, staring silently—and disapprovingly—with invisible eyes on the three travelers. Mariel shook herself. This was silly and childish, and it came from reading too many tales about spooky forests like this one.

"I think I'm getting paranoid," she muttered to herself. The twitching ears of Simeon and Anna let Mariel know they'd heard, but they made no reply. They were also looking around, seemingly as disconcerted as Mariel was.

They proceeded with caution. The dreary woods were eerily silent—so silent that Mariel could hear every footfall from herself and her companions, and every heartbeat pounded in her ears. She almost fancied she could hear the heartbeats of Anna and Simeon, too.

Suddenly there was a wild shriek, and a shadow swooped down from the higher tree branches. All three companions instinctively cowered. Mariel caught a better glimpse of it as it flew away from them.

"A...condor? I think?" Mariel craned back and forth, trying to get a better view of the bird through the trees. "It *is* a condor. It's...it's huge!" Suddenly she was chuckling under her breath. "For a minute, I thought it was one of those pterodactyls. I feel like I've wandered into Jurassic Park."

Not knowing what Jurassic Park was, Anna and Simeon failed to catch the humor in the remark. They trotted obligingly after Mariel, who picked up her pace and marched with renewed boldness into the Avian Jungle. The condor made her feel a little bolder, and she tried to tell herself that it was the huge bird she'd sensed watching them—not the trees.

Only Anna looked back at the sunny archway, shining like the opening of a tunnel as it shrunk behind them. She shuddered. When they rounded a corner, it disappeared altogether, leaving them to wander through the oppressive gloom. Mariel took no notice. Her sight was arrested by an elaborate water park which opened up like an island amid the gray trees, complete with dancing fountains and impressive waterfalls. The edges were thick with cattails and reeds. Nervous frogs hopped over the lily pads.

And no wonder they were nervous. Predators were everywhere. But such glorious predators! Proud peacocks, their blue-green tails fanned to their fullest, strolled arrogantly about the immaculate grounds, pecking here and there and pretending to ignore the drab gray females, who were shy and diminutive by comparison. Pink flamingos and showy cranes stood at the edges of small pools, lazing about and half-dozing while balanced on one leg. Snowy swans glided over the water's surface, small gray puffs of feathers perched on their backs or swimming at their sides. On the shore, nests of mallards were hidden in the reeds, and one mother was raising her voice.

"Merciful heavens, look at this ugly duckling, will you? He'll never amount to anything!"

Mariel flinched at the insult levied against the duck's own chick and looked away, then gasped and stopped cold. "Why...how dreadful!"

For there, before her, was a sight that pierced her to the heart. A pure white dove sat perfectly still, his head lowered sorrowfully, in a tiny cage barely large enough to accommodate him. An enormous padlock was over the little door. Longingly, he watched blackbirds flying in the surrounding forest, and a flock of crows stood near, guffawing and making fun of the young dove, who accepted his sad fate with tears in his eyes and lowered wings.

"Oh...it's not fair!" whimpered Mariel, her lips trembling at the awful sight. "They've...robbed him of his freedom!"

Simeon and Anna looked on, their faces grim. "Marcus was right," Simeon said finally. Then he added, very quietly,

"That dove is like an extension of the Zookeeper himself. They locked him away because he's the biggest threat to the new government."

"He's not the only one they've locked away," muttered Anna, directing their attention to a point beyond the dove cage. "Look."

Mariel recognized a tiger trap when she saw one, and this tiger trap was packed with twenty or thirty bald eagles. Their striking white heads contrasted sharply with their darker brown plumage. All of them bore the same dejected demeanor as the white dove, and one gazed dully at the gargantuan padlock securing their door and preventing them from taking the skies. A second tiger trap housed the largest bald eagle Mariel had ever seen; he dwarfed the other eagles and rivaled Mariel herself in height.

"Whatever did they do wrong?" Mariel wanted to know.

"Hush," ordered Simeon. He glanced around at the other birds meaningfully; none of them seemed to take notice of the three travelers. "Forget everything you saw here. Walk on and say no more."

It's impossible to forget, thought Mariel ruefully, but she plodded down the path after Simeon. Her heavy feet dragged, and her heart ached for the dove, especially. There was something perfect and innocent about him, and the cruelty of locking him away was beyond her. They treated him like a dangerous criminal, and he was a dove—just a dove.

Anna butted her muzzle against Mariel's back. "Buck up," she encouraged. "Think of...our destination."

Mariel's fingers wormed into her jeans' pocket and touched the scroll there. It worked. Sorrow was replaced by a fresh fire of determination. As soon as the Zookeeper was back, he would set the captives free.

They rounded another bend, leaving the water park

behind. The forest gloom closed over them again. The bird-song which had serenaded them since they left the Sign of the Times now exploded around them in full volume as songbirds of every species and size gave voice to their never-ending joy—chirping and twittering and warbling and squawking. When the birds saw the three visitors, the noise level increased. Within minutes, it was almost deafening, and they were flying thick as bats across the walkway.

Mariel clapped her hands over her ears. Anna and Simeon flattened their ears against their necks as all three of them stumbled to a halt. A young blond fellow dressed in tan khakis came running out from inside the bole of a giant tree and glared up at the chaos.

"QUIET!"

There was a rush of wings. The songbirds departed the tree branches in a wild collage of bright color.

Shaking his head, the ranger leveled his brown-eyed gaze on the company. "Sorry. They always get excited when we have visitors. They think it's feeding time."

"Little vultures!" Mariel remarked in mild amusement, lowering her hands.

The ranger chuckled, his stare included Anna and Simeon. "That's about accurate. They're spoiled rotten, every last one of them." He returned his searching gaze to Mariel. "I'm Rick, by the way."

Something, like a whispered warning, tugged at Mariel's mind. He could've been the one who locked away the dove and the eagles. "Mars," Mariel returned shortly, shaking his proffered hand.

Rick studied her with interest. "That's an unusual name."

Mariel shrugged. "You're not the first to have pointed it out." Pivoting, she gestured to Anna and Simeon. "This is—"

"Simon," put in Simeon quickly.

Anna smiled, a trifle forced. "Nina."

"Well! Welcome to the Avian Jungle," said Rick magnanimously, but his grin didn't quite reach his brown eyes. "I'm afraid there aren't as many rangers here as there once were. They're all…cleaning up after the donkeys in another part of the Menagerie."

Simeon pricked his ears. "We've heard it's gotten messy on the Other Side."

"*Very* messy," Rick corrected, relaxing his guard slightly. "Whether you're heading to the City of Gold or all the way to the Capital, the path through the Avian Jungle is definitely the shortest route now. Though I should warn you that, due to the lack of rangers to go around, Reptilian Paradise has been left completely unattended."

"Is that wise?" wondered Anna with a tremor in her voice.

Rick swept a hand through his blond hair. "Unfortunately, it can't be helped, wise or not. Things are that bad on the other side of the Menagerie. But at least I've got one good assistant, and my lovely wife Kim, to help me out here," he added, glancing back at the tree from which he'd first emerged. An ornate lamp was fixed into the side of it, illuminated brightly against the dense tree-induced gloom, near a cleverly disguised door with a gold handle. It reminded Mariel of Robin Hood's mythical hideout tree in Sherwood Forest, and she suddenly wanted to see the inside of it very badly.

At that moment, Simeon had other ideas. "Well, it's been a pleasure, but we should get going."

Rick chuckled, but there was a speculative gleam in his eyes that unsettled Mariel's stomach. "Of course. Enjoy the sights." He glanced at the canopy above.

As if at his bidding, a peregrine falcon left his perch and swooped low over the path towards the company, pulling up at the last second and rising again into the sky, his lordly gaze never deigning to fall upon the lowly mortals below. Mariel watched, enraptured, as he soared away, the light breeze ruffling his feathers. The wind of his passage brushed against her face.

"What must it be like, to have wings?" she wondered aloud, stricken suddenly by a poetic sense of awe. "To leave the world and all its petty concerns behind, to defy gravity, to—"

"*Gravitas!*"

The harsh screeching voice came from somewhere above them. Rick paled. "Oh, no, you didn't—"

"*Gravitas! Gravitas!*"

Mariel's blue eyes went wide as she suddenly remembered the sign. "I said gravity, not—"

"*GRAVITAS! GRAVITAS! GRAVITAS!*"

Stumbling backwards, Mariel frantically searched the treetops. Branches filled with parrots—African grays, scarlet macaws with blue and yellow wings, bright green Amazons, and many others Mariel couldn't put names to—were clustered there, and soon even more were flapping in to join the chorus. Rick put a hand to his head momentarily in despair, then raced over to another tree, opening the small door built into its bark. He hauled out a heavy sack of birdseed and hurled handfuls of it at the parrots, pelting them.

It had no effect whatsoever. They went on wailing. "*GRAVITAS! GRAVITAS!*"

"Get out of here!" Rick shouted to Mariel's company. "Quick, before...just quick!"

They lost no time in obeying. The painfully loud cacophony faded as they ran down the path.

Simeon glanced over his withers and snorted. "Uh-oh, we're too late..."

A black cloud covered the sun. Mariel whirled and saw that the cloud was composed of hundreds of vultures, all swooping down to land in the treetops and on the ground near the three travelers like a blanket of tar. The buzzards closed in on them, squinting with mean yellow eyes in their fleshy pink heads. Mariel's nostrils quivered at the faintly sickening odor the scavengers brought with them.

They began talking all at once.

"How does it feel to know that you've been the cause of a major disturbance?"

"Did you say the word 'gravity' on purpose, knowing it would set off a new round of 'gravitas'?"

"How many years have you known the parrots?"

"How long do you think it will be before the Avian Jungle is back to normal?"

Mariel was too bewildered to answer. Accusations wrapped in the form of questions were being flung at her from every side until she couldn't make them out anymore. They became an unintelligible garble of language mixed with the harsh cries of advancing vultures. Frightened, Mariel backed against Simeon and clutched handfuls of his mane.

Simeon and Anna pressed close to her, and they began to move out of the black ring. "No comment. No comment at this time," was Simeon's firm mantra. "Move aside, please."

The vultures were reluctant to move. But when Simeon's enormous hoof landed on one buzzard's wing, an unearthly shrieking broke out. Dozens of vultures fluttered away, clearing a few feet of the path, and Simeon and Anna took advantage of it. They broke into a swift canter, and no bird dared stand in their way. They parted like the Red Sea. With Mariel sandwiched between them, they dashed out beyond a second archway, over which a sign read: *We hope you enjoyed your visit! Come again soon!*

Sunlight enveloped them as they burst out of the jungle. The buzzards didn't follow, but Mariel kept on running with her two friends. Glancing over her shoulder, the girl gasped softly. One lone vulture was flying into the clear skies, headed for the right side of the Menagerie.

Anna also saw him leave and picked up her pace. "Time is running out!" she cried.

CHAPTER
TWELVE

They couldn't keep up their blistering pace for long. Once the Avian Jungle faded from sight, they slowed and walked on in silence. Mariel rested a hand on Simeon's back, trying to catch her breath.

The silence didn't last long.

"Hey-hey, lookie here, another biped! I git three points."

Mariel glanced to her left and found three fat pigs, lazily

wallowing in a muddy ditch beside the road. She hadn't seen them right away because they were covered in mud.

"No, you only git *two* points, because it's one point per leg."

"Yeah, but there should be a bonus, 'cause true bipeds are rare."

"Whatever," piped up the third, "but I got you both beat, 'cause I saw the horse first. Oh, lookie, an' a llama!"

A flurry of protests from the other two pigs was interrupted when Anna's head snapped around. "How do you know my name?"

The pig blinked at her. "What's your name?"

Mariel set a hand on Anna's soft neck and shot her a quelling glance, then pulled the map from her pack and studied it carefully, ignoring the pigs' continuing conversation.

"Dude, drop it, 'cause there's no extra points for knowing a name. What's in a name, anyways?"

They laughed at the quote and rolled over in the mud, kicking up their hooves and lazing on their backs in the sunshine. Simeon turned his gray head towards them.

"You'd best be warned," he said to them. "There are wolves roaming about. It isn't wise to linger here."

"Ah, wolves." One of the pigs splashed his cloven hoof in the mud, unconcerned. "That just means more points, right, fellas?"

There was chuckling and a hearty chorus of agreement. Another one of the pigs eyed Simeon and wiggled his hoof slyly. "A-ha, a-ha, I git your little game. A wolf, and we're the three little pigs, right?" He grinned at his companions, and all at once they began to sing *Who's Afraid of the Big Bad Wolf* quite dreadfully. Then they broke out in coarse laughter, grunting and squealing.

Anna trotted to the other side of the path and hid behind Simeon's huge frame, looking angry and ready to cry all at the same time. Simeon put his nose up to her as the crude pig noises faded behind them.

There was a bend in the path approaching, flanked thickly on both sides by windblown willows. Mariel was concentrating so hard on the map that when the world began to tremble beneath her feet, she almost didn't notice, until the clatter of hopping pebbles against the flagstones became audible. Anna and Simeon had stopped, their hooves planted and their ears swiveling nervously. Mariel moved backwards and cowered between them.

"What...an earthquake?" she cried, clinging to Simeon's mane.

"Something's coming," whispered Anna, frightened.

Through the trees, Mariel caught a glimpse of something huge and gray moving in their direction at an alarming rate. There was a horrible trumpeting blast and a wail of despair. Every step the monster took shook Mariel to her very bones, but she was too paralyzed to move. There was nowhere to go, either. The ditches on either side of the road were brimming with mud. Simeon gripped Mariel by the back of the shirt and half-dragged her off the road, ankle-deep into the mud, and Anna stumbled after them as a full-grown elephant rounded the corner, galloping for all he was worth and trumpeting, his white-rimmed eyes rolling in terror.

"It's coming! It's coming!" he shouted inanely to the three companions, who were standing miserably in the mud and staring. "Run!"

Flapping his great big ears, he barreled on. His thumping footsteps and the accompanying earthquake faded with his departure. Mariel gasped and looked at the curving path with some trepidation. Anna and Simeon stood with pricked ears, also gazing intently.

For a long time, there was nothing. Then, presently, there

was a faint *tap, tap, tap* on the flagstones. Mariel shifted her feet in the thick mud, stopping immediately when she felt her shoes tug as if to come off, and that's when she saw the creature.

It was a tiny whiskered creature in a miniature black suit and a silk-lined black cape. A mouse.

The mouse strode up to them, tapping his polished mahogany walking stick at each dignified step, and pausing before the muddy crew he swept off his top hat and bowed.

"A good afternoon to you!" Rising again, he settled his hat onto his gray head. "I say," he declared in a decidedly British accent, pulling out a tiny gold pocket watch and studying it, "It seems a bit late to be indulging in a mud fight by the side of the road, ay, chaps? Dueling is not openly permitted, but it is a bit less messy than fighting in the mud."

All three of them stood there, blinking at the ridiculous mouse. The mouse blinked back through half-lidded eyes as if they were equally ridiculous. At that moment, Mariel felt ridiculous, standing in a pool of mud with a horse and a llama and carrying on a conversation with a proud little mouse dressed to the nines.

"We weren't...fighting, sir mouse," ventured Mariel.

The mouse drew himself up taller—if that were possible—and twitched his stylish cravat. It was already perfect, so Mariel could only imagine the gesture was designed to draw attention to it. "That's *gentle* mouse, dear lady," he corrected her, somewhat put out.

"Gentle mouse?" Mariel repeated incredulously. The notion was laughable, but the little mouse was so deadly serious that it didn't strike Mariel as entirely comical.

"Most assuredly." With a superior sniff, the gentle mouse hooked his cane over his forearm and adjusted the costly lace at his sleeves. "I come from a long line of gentle mice. I am formally known as Sir Francis Conrad Joseph Drake Von Krogman, the Earl of Cheese. But you may simply address me as Sir Francis."

There was another awkward silence. Then, at the same moment, all three companions suddenly began to slog their way out of the ditch. There was something wrong with marinating in mud while addressing the Earl of Cheese himself. He might have been small, but he radiated a great deal of power, wealth and influence.

"May I ask what is coming, Sir Francis?" Mariel asked, shifting her feet. She was fully conscious of her mud-crusted jeans, but Anna and Simeon seemed oblivious, staring intently at Sir Francis.

"I do beg your pardon," returned the mouse with a little sniff.

"An elephant ran by only a moment ago in a great hurry. He said something was coming."

It seemed to Mariel that the Earl bit back a smirk. He ran an elegant paw down one of his long whiskers. "That would be me, I'm afraid," he answered in a grave tone of faux modesty. "That's not so surprising, really. Elephants run at the looming specter of their own shadows. They're always predicting the end of civilization as we know it and prophesying doom and destruction on all of society," he drawled in a bored tone, "just because of a few modern advancements in thinking. Poppycock!" The word burst out of him so suddenly that Mariel jumped. "Here we are on a fine day, having a pleasant conversation without the slightest hint of societal degeneration. Business is prospering and the cheese markets are booming. Sad lot, those pachyderms, really," he muttered, shaking his little head. "Elephants are so very short-sighted. Little wonder, then, that they run when they see me approaching."

"Well, you're really not so terrifying," said Mariel in puzzlement, garnering a sharp look from Sir Francis. "I just mean," she amended hastily, "that there are much nastier creatures one could meet."

"Mm." Miffed, the Earl turned a haughty shoulder to them, as if they were no longer worth his time, and checked his gold pocketwatch. Snapping it shut, he dropped it in a pocket. "Good morning!" He made as if to continue on his way.

"A moment, if you please." Simeon stepped forward for the first time. "Did you pass through Reptilian Paradise?"

Sir Francis made a great show of acquiescing to this interruption in his busy life with much reluctance, as if he hardly had time for mere peasants. He looked over his shoulder and gazed at Simeon through the corner of one half-lidded eye. "I certainly did."

The workhorse blew softly through his nostrils and carefully worded his question. "Is it...well, safe?"

"Most certainly!" The tiny cane came down with an emphatic tap. "And don't you let anyone tell you otherwise. Those reptiles do more good for the future of the Menagerie than all the idiotic bureaucrats in the Capital put together. And now, I must be going. Good morning!"

Whirling his little black cape, the Earl of Cheese strode away. The *tap, tap, tap* of his miniature cane faded with him.

Mariel exchanged puzzled glances with her friends. Without a word, they hurried down the road, an even greater urgency upon them. Each was wrapped in her or his own private musings concerning the place they were collectively about to enter, but none bothered sharing.

And so it was with great trepidation that they came to a pale-colored adobe city, made entirely of sun-dried mud. It reminded Mariel of a long windowless tunnel. The entrance was an archway upon which were carved the words *Reptilian*

Paradise. A huge iron bell topped the elaborate front of the city, swinging idly in the breeze but making no sound. Gray pigeons flapped about the belfry.

They crossed the threshold. Inside the adobe building, the sunlight was abruptly cut off and relegated to a few narrow shafts from holes in the ceiling, which acted as open skylights to let in both sunshine and rainwater. The few boulders in the otherwise bare, sand-covered floor were positioned directly beneath those roof holes. The shade was a welcome relief, and Mariel suddenly realized, when she pressed a hand to her warm cheeks, that she was getting sunburnt. The air carried with it a slight sickening odor and Mariel saw Simeon's nostrils quivering. Her shoes crunched the sand grains that encroached into the flagstone pathway, along with a few pigeon feathers.

"Rather quiet in here," murmured Mariel, just to break the oppressive silence. Her voice echoed eerily in the dark. Then, even more lowly, she added, "There doesn't seem to be anyone about."

"Ah, but there isss."

Mariel screamed and leaped sideways. Anna and Simeon reared up in surprise as a long, black creature slithered out from behind a boulder, largely hidden in the shadows. An ominous rattling sent a jolt of alarm rocketing down Mariel's spine.

"Who are you?" Mariel gasped.

There was a low, dark chuckle from the creature. "The Keeper of the Gate," he hissed in a silky voice that was chillingly smooth. "But the real question isss," and he suddenly crawled upwards onto the nearest boulder and coiled his splotchy brown body in the spotlight of sunshine, lifting his flat head to a greater height, "who are *you?*"

Mariel was speechless. She'd never seen a rattlesnake before, let alone come this close to one! The snake's tail began to rattle threateningly again, and Mariel started. "I… I… I'm Mariel," she stammered, too frightened to remember not to give her real name.

"Marrr-iel." There was something sickening about the rattlesnake's tone, and the way he looked at her with slitted yellow eyes shook Mariel's courage to its roots. "And what would you be doing here?"

"Just passing through." Simeon regained his courage first and stepped beside Mariel, with Anna hiding behind him. Mariel quickly nodded, her eyes never leaving the snake.

"I sssee." The gatekeeper flicked his tongue and leveled an evil glare on Simeon. "There isss no sssuch thing as 'just passsing through.' You have a dessstination. What isss it?"

The question was directed at Mariel, but Simeon took it upon himself to answer. "The City of Gold."

The rattlesnake shot him an irritated look. "I wasssn't talking to you, horssse."

"I'm leading this group," replied Simeon evenly. "Now what right do you have to detain us?"

"I make my own rulesss," hissed the rattlesnake, shaking his tail in mounting anger and raising his squat head higher. He weaved slightly from side to side, positioned to strike at any moment. "You have entered the domain of the reptilesss, and you will follow our rulesss!"

"The Menagerie is free to all creatures," stated Simeon calmly, his dark eyes fixed on the snake. "This pathway has existed long before plans for the Reptilian Paradise were even drawn up. Now let us pass!"

"No!" Furious, the snake slithered down from his perch and coiled up in the middle of the pathway, rattling his tail and weaving his head from side to side. He flicked his forked tongue at them. "I sssay. You will *not* passs! Leave now, or elsssse!"

Simeon backed up a hoof, and then another. Anna and Mariel moved with him, casting glances between the work-horse and the deadly rattlesnake.

"No need for all that," muttered Simeon quietly. "Good day." So saying, he turned his tail on the snake and led the small party out of the adobe building, back into the blinding daylight.

Mariel glanced over her shoulder when they were out of earshot, then stared at Simeon, incredulous. "How could you back down? We have to get through…"

"I know." The corner of Simeon's mouth was quirked in a dry smile. "He won't stop us this time. Mariel, on my back, now."

"But…"

"*Now!*"

Mariel swallowed hard, then boosted herself onto the dappled gray back, clutching fistfuls of white mane. Anna watched them, shifting hooves nervously.

"All right," said Simeon when the girl was settled. "Now, let's make a run for it."

Satisfied that they were gone, the rattlesnake was shaking his tail to himself, flicking his forked tongue in sheer pleasure. He'd won again. He liked triumphing over the small-minded mammalian creatures. Reptiles *were* superior, by far, but warm-bloods didn't know that. Not yet. But they soon would—when reptiles ruled over the Menagerie.

Grinning, the snake was about to settle under his rock and doze for a while, the glow of the sun's warmth still pulsing through his sleek brown body, when he picked up the faint but delicious tendrils of a small rodent's scent.

"Moussse," he hissed softly to himself, pleased. He was in the mood to celebrate his moral victory with a snack. Flicking his tongue, he abandoned his hiding spot and slithered along the side of the pathway. The moment his scales made contact with the flagstones, the whole world began to tremble.

Whipping around, the snake shook his tail in violent fury at the sight of the gray workhorse plunging into the shadows of Reptilian Paradise at full gallop, his hoof feathers flying like white flames while the girl clung to his back in the desperate charge. The little llama was cantering right behind him.

"I told you to ssstay out!" growled the snake, hastily taking his place before the horse—and paling. Those killer hooves were enormous, and death was written in the horse's blazing eyes.

But the snake refused to back down. Curling his deadly body, he bared his poisonous fangs and poised himself to strike.

He lashed out at Simeon's forehoof. He missed. He had time for one loud hiss of frustration before Simeon's hind hooves came down and crushed his head. Instantly, the rattlesnake flopped over on the pathway, his limp tail silent. Simeon checked his stride, glancing back at Anna. She gazed back at him with wide eyes, still running to keep up with him. A pale-faced Mariel was just praying she wouldn't fall off.

The trio stopped, gasping for breath—more from the adrenaline of the moment than exertion. Mariel's fingers were embedded so deeply in Simeon's mane that she worried she'd never untangle them. She started to sit upright—and paused.

"What's that?" she whispered.

From all around them, there came a faint noise—like the distant rushing of a river, or the soft buzz of bumblebees around a hive. Anna nervously huddled close to Simeon, and they searched everywhere for the source of the sound. In the semidarkness, they couldn't see anything alive.

And then one phrase became startlingly clear to Mariel. "They killed the gatekeeper! The gatekeeper is dead!" Dozens of tiny, raspy voices took up the cry. Something black rushed swiftly up one of the adobe walls, and Mariel smothered a scream. It was some kind of lizard probably, but it had vanished out one of the roof holes and was, even now, somewhere above them.

Ghostly whispers echoed faintly around them. "They shouldn't have done that… They won't get away with thisss…"

The realization that hundreds of reptilian eyes might be looking down on them from above, even now, chilled Mariel's blood. Her wide eyes slashed between shafts of sunlight, and she fancied she could hear the faint clicking of reptilian claws on the adobe ceiling.

"Spies… Kill them… Tell the boas! Get the boas! Make them pay!"

A little whimper broke from Anna. "Dear Zookeeper…"

"Hang on!" hollered Simeon, and he broke into another jolting breakneck gallop. Mariel cried out and leaned low along his strong neck, his creamy mane flicking back at her cheeks like miniature whips. And all the while, her eyes were adjusting to the dim interior of Reptilian Paradise, and a shock of horror ran through her when she saw entire carcasses of dead creatures picked to the bones strewn about either side of the pathway. Now she recognized the sickening smell of death all around her. And from those morbid ribcages emerged snakes—cobras and sidewinders and coral snakes and more rattlesnakes, until it looked like a boiling sea of dark oil in the muted sunlight.

Anna cantered bravely at Simeon's side, her dark eyes full of terror. Then she screamed. "Look out!"

Down from the roof suddenly dropped the biggest snake Mariel had ever seen, its huge head swinging in space as its slitted eyes flicked back and forth and finally settled on the approaching company. Simeon swerved wildly. Mariel almost lost her balance and struggled to hold on. Then she looked over her shoulder as the snake landed on the ground with a thud behind them, its huge body coiling around nothing. Her heart pounding, Mariel turned her gaze forward and stopped breathing when four monstrous snake heads came down with frightening suddenness, swinging like giant pendulums as they searched for their prey—and one by one dropped down at the horse in an air attack.

Simeon dodged back and forth between them as they fell and curled like monster tires. Mariel couldn't keep up with Simeon's agile twists. She felt his strong back slip from beneath her thighs, and she gave a cry as she hurtled through the air and came down hard on her tailbone.

Stars exploded in her head, and the world stopped. "Ow…"

Something thick and clammy instantly wrapped around her waist. Mariel had a glimpse of a horrid reptilian head as it moved around her, evil intent gleaming in its yellow eyes. Galvanized into motion, Mariel screamed and pushed her hands desperately against the hard scaly body, fighting for breath. But it was too late. It had her firmly in its grasp. Mariel shoved at it, but it was like wrenching at a tree trunk. "Simeon!"

Simeon wheeled, his hooves sliding against the flagstones, and gave his head a vicious shake. "Run, Anna! Go!" he commanded, but he was coming back to get Mariel.

Mariel was suddenly more afraid of *him* than the boa constrictor slowly wrapping itself around her; he was like a dark gray thunderstorm, and his mane snapped like white lightning. Simeon gathered himself and leaped over another dropped boa constrictor. He dashed behind the girl, going for the snake's head, and all at once his fury was unleashed on Mariel's captor. Mariel could feel the boa constrictor start violently and go into convulsions, and she knew a battle was raging somewhere behind her, but she couldn't see Simeon anymore.

The muscles in the gigantic body clenched spasmodically around Mariel's ribcage, and she cried out in pain and terror as it squeezed the air from her lungs. A steady hum built in her ears. "Simeon… Simeon!" she whimpered desperately, pitting all her strength against the creature's. She kicked at it—it felt like a rock—and tried to wriggle her way to freedom. Somewhere behind her, Simeon was roaring and his hooves clattered fiercely against the flagstone pathway.

But Mariel was running out of oxygen. The boa constrictor managed to get another loop around her and tightened it even more until Mariel grew dizzy and her vision clouded. Her struggles became useless, frantic flailings, slowly getting weaker. The snake gave one last massive jerk of its body, and the pressure against Mariel's ribs was overwhelming. Any second, she expected her bones to crack in the merciless coils.

Mariel gave a faint cry and blacked out.

CHAPTER
THIRTEEN

"Mariel? Mariel, wake up…"

As if from far away, Mariel heard someone calling her name. She took a deep breath—and groaned. Her ribs hurt. The pain roused her from her unconsciousness, and she opened her eyes. Everything was blurry.

"Where am I?" came her strangely distorted voice. "Am I…dead?"

"Not yet."

Something soft nuzzled her cheek and Mariel turned towards it, blinking away the last fringes of fuzz over her vision. "Anna?"

The llama smiled, clear relief in her teary eyes. "Little one, it's good to see you awake." Mariel saw Anna swallow, though her smile never faded. "I thought we were going to lose you."

Mariel frowned, wondering what to make of that statement. Suddenly everything came rushing back, and she sat up—too fast—and put a hand gingerly on her aching ribs. She moaned. "Where's Simeon?"

"Over there," answered Anna softly, nodding her muzzle towards the sleeping horse in one corner of the room.

Mariel swung her feet to the floor, ignoring Anna's half-hearted protests and her own sore body. She knelt beside the great horse and gazed down at him. The terrible fury radiating from him the night before was gone, and in its place was the gentle giant Mariel had come to know and love. So many feelings stirred inside her. Simeon had risked his life to save her, and somehow he'd succeeded. She owed her life to him—again. She was grateful and awed and humbled and mortified, all at the same time.

She watched the peaceful rise and fall of his sides in slumber, and she placed a hand tenderly on his neck. "Thank you," she whispered.

Mariel was aware that Anna had moved behind her and was gazing over Mariel's shoulder at him. "Let him sleep, for now," she urged. "Come get something to eat."

Hot cream of broccoli soup had never tasted so good to Mariel. Despite her ordeal and the resulting soreness and bruises, Mariel's appetite was quite healthy. She felt strength returning to her with every spoonful.

"How did…I mean, how did I end up here?" Mariel wondered presently.

"You don't remember?"

Mariel shook her head.

"Not surprising, really," the llama mused. "You were only half-conscious. Simeon killed the boa constrictor shortly before you passed out," Anna explained, nudging the basket of warm croissants within Mariel's reach. "It seemed determined to kill you, even in its death throes. I didn't run when Simeon told me to." She smiled innocently. "I never listen when he says things like that."

Mariel chuckled in between bites and slathered a thick layer of honey butter over a croissant. "What about the other snakes I saw coming out of everywhere?"

"Well, Simeon kind of trampled them."

"Did any of them…get him?" Mariel paused with her knife in the air and cast a worried glance at the sleeping horse.

Anna nodded. "They did. Luckily they only bit him in the hooves, or so he said, and those hooves are almost as tough as his head. He killed a great many of them, and together we managed to get you out of there."

"But if I was unconscious, how…?"

Anna interrupted with a smile. "Because you weren't unconscious, dear. You came to after a moment and crawled onto Simeon's back."

"Strange… I don't have any memory of that," remarked Mariel in bewilderment, her croissant momentarily forgotten as she stared off into space and racked her mind for any residual shred of mental evidence to confirm Anna's story. She could hardly believe she'd come through all that alive. She remembered only a terrifying collage of reptiles pouring out of everywhere and boiling towards them like an angry sea of pure venom.

"Not necessarily strange. It happens after one is locked in a fight for survival."

It was disturbing to Mariel nonetheless. She felt as if she'd lost something vitally important. Rising, she wandered to the open window and looked out—and gasped.

Everything was gold, glittering and blindingly bright in the sunlight. The very air was intoxicating, thick with golden perfume as it brushed through Mariel's dark hair. The road was paved with gold bricks, the towering buildings gleamed gold—especially the twin skyscrapers near the gate, Mariel noticed, leaning over the windowpane to see as far as she could. There was an enormous gold fountain in the golden city square, where statues of gold Cupids cavorted in the water and among beds of yellow flowers.

Mariel had never seen a donkey with pierced ears before, but there was one among the crowd wearing giant gold hoop earrings, as well as a gold silk scarf. Her hooves were painted gold, and her tail was braided with shimmering gold ribbon. The creatures surrounding her on the busy pathway were similarly bedecked, each wearing as much gold silk and gold jewelry as it possibly could.

"We're in the City of Gold," Anna confirmed, a trace of amusement lurking in her voice.

"I...wouldn't have guessed," Mariel breathed, bedazzled.

"Seeing is believing," said a deep voice behind her. "Maybe we should go down for a closer—"

Mariel whirled with a squeal. "Simeon!" She threw her arms around the great workhorse's neck, then softened her embrace immediately, her face buried in Simeon's coarse, creamy mane.

Chuffing affectionately, Simeon nuzzled her shoulder. "Equally delighted, Mariel. But time marches on without us. Shall we go?"

Moments later, they were on those crowded streets, with sunlight winking at them from the brilliant golden surfaces.

The creatures walking past them were absorbed in their own business and hustled past the little group of three, seeming not to notice them at all. Mariel kept a hand in Simeon's mane so she could walk along and look around without losing track of him.

It suddenly occurred to Mariel that the creatures around her were either in their prime or just past it, mostly proud and haughty animals. There weren't any young creatures that Mariel could see. She found that a little odd and turned to ask Simeon about it.

"Here there, little lady!" called out a voice, and, upon turning, Mariel's eyes widened. A tall, fat merchant with a wide toothy grin, wearing an outfit made entirely of gold silk— from his bloomers to his turban—was smiling at her, standing before a cart piled with mountains of gold apples. He handed one to her.

"Oh, I...how much does it cost?" hedged Mariel, belatedly realizing she'd fallen into the skilled clutches of a professional salesman.

Chuckling, the merchant stuck his thumbs in the wide sash winding around his generous waist. "Not a penny! You must not be from around here," he observed then, still grinning. "These apples grow like money on trees, and they are quite free." He laughed openly at Mariel's expression of amazed bewilderment. "'Tis a paradise, seemingly, no? Well, it is," he answered his own question. "My orchards flourish not far beyond the city gates, and the Golden Palace pays me a handsome sum to distribute these to all and sundry. Not that many around here qualify as sundry, mind you."

Mariel looked up from studying her apple, which was surprisingly soft and pliant beneath her probing fingers despite its incredible shine. "I thought you said they were free," she remarked, bewildered.

"Course they are!" he thundered, laughing again. He lifted his face to the sun, his whole being radiating his obvious opinion that life was good. "Comes right out of the taxes, this does."

"Well," wondered Mariel, glancing at her apple again with increasing puzzlement, "if the inhabitants have to pay for the apples in such a roundabout fashion, why not just let them buy the apples the old-fashioned way?"

A derisive snort was almost more eloquent than his following speech. "It's progress, little lady," he said, holding out apples to Anna and Simeon as well, which they accepted with polite nods and promptly chomped into. Mariel's attention was temporarily diverted by the sight of a fat porcupine eagerly spearing apples on his quills until his entire back was covered with them. Well satisfied with himself, the greedy miser trundled off, unaware of how ridiculous he looked—and unaware of other creatures reaching over either stealthy paws or surreptitious muzzles to pick off an apple or two, just because those golden treats were conveniently located beneath their noses on a mobile palette.

Returning her frown to the merchant, Mariel narrowed her eyes at him. "It's more than that, I imagine," she began, but she was cut off by a hard shove in the back from Simeon's muzzle.

The workhorse swallowed his apple and nodded gravely to the merchant. "Thank you," he said as if to leave. He deliberately pushed his strong shoulder against the girl, forcing her to move away.

Once the company was back on the road, Simeon shot her a stern glance and lowered his voice. "Don't engage the natives in conversation if you don't have to," he told her firmly. "It's unwise. It's particularly unwise if you're about to point out something that could work to his disadvantage. I assume you were about to say that these apples cost the inhabitants of this city more with their 'progressive' methods. You're right, of course."

Mariel stared at him in dawning comprehension. Then she cast a dark glower at her apple. "I can't eat this."

"Why not?" wondered Anna.

"Because *my* tax dollars aren't going back to the merchant. So technically it's stealing."

"Technically, it's a flaw in the system," Simeon pointed out. "One of many, but one which he finds particularly advantageous. The Golden Palace obviously pays him a handsome sum for those apples, so he doesn't care whose hands they fall into."

When Mariel remained dubious, Anna nuzzled her elbow. "Think of it as a gift from the entire Menagerie. They don't know it yet, but they're helping you complete…er…this most important journey."

Reluctantly, Mariel accepted that and bit into the apple. At once her blue eyes lit up, and she took another eager bite, which seemed to melt in her mouth. She licked every last particle of apple pulp from the core as if it were a popsicle and tossed the core by the wayside, proclaiming it the best apple she'd ever had while wishing she could have another.

Just then, a murmur of excitement rippled through the creatures. Lilting melodies of flutes and golden bells reached Mariel's ears, and standing on her tiptoes she craned this way and that to peer over the heads of the masses. In a moment, she saw a beautiful golden canopy, its many tassels swaying merrily at each step, and the animals before it parted to make way, each bowing its gold-adorned head low. The canopy was unlike anything Mariel had ever seen. Its rectangular floor was covered in plush gold carpet, and it rolled along on carriage wheels. The gold silk curtains were partially open, for now, but they could easily be drawn shut for further privacy. As it was, they were loosely pulled back to four corner posts and still obscured Mariel's view of the occupant.

As the sumptuous float came closer and more animals moved aside, Mariel saw that it was drawn by what looked like a strange reddish-colored rhinoceros—with seven heads. Mariel felt a terrible wave of dread, staring as all seven gold-horned heads bobbed and moved with minds of their own. The head in the center was by far the most impressive, with four thick, golden horns, instead of just one, reminiscent of a crown. Its golden harness jangled, draped with garlands of gold chains, bells, and flowers. An entourage of dark-skinned menservants wearing gold silk—tunics, turbans, bloomers and golden slippers that curled at the toe—came after the canopy, playing golden instruments and creating beautiful music in their wake.

"It's like something out of Arabian Nights," Mariel breathed.

"We'd better move," murmured Simeon, nudging the girl with his nose.

The three companions stood by the side of the path. With an effort of will, Mariel shut her gaping jaw. The squinty black eyes of the beast seemed to her calculating and mean, and as he drew even with Mariel, three of its heads turned and looked straight at her. Mariel cringed under their searching gaze and looked back to the canopy. The breeze blew the silky gold curtains further aside, and the sight took Mariel's breath away.

A beautiful golden-haired princess, clothed in rich purple and bedecked with more gold jewelry than Mariel had ever seen on one person, lounged on gold cushions and gazed into a mirror, seemingly enraptured with whatever she found there. And no wonder! Her skin was almost luminescent and the color of dark gold. Once in a while, she touched her long golden tresses, which were flowing with gold charms trailing from her ornate crown. All around her were fragrant spreads of mysterious pear-shaped fruits, and a golden goblet sat near her elbow. She laid aside the mirror briefly and was just reaching for the goblet when her dark eyes met Mariel's blank stare, and the princess's blood-red lips curved into a smooth smile that was at once alluring and predatory.

"Hello, dear." Her melodious voice was enchanting, and Mariel felt a little dizzy.

"Er, hello," she returned somewhat nervously, bobbing an awkward curtsy and backing up against Simeon.

The princess leaned forward. "Baby, do stop." And the beast came to a halt, all seven of its horned heads snorting and tossing. The nearest head craned around to glare at Mariel.

But Mariel didn't notice. It was as if the golden princess had cast a spell over her—and the other animals along the pathway, who were staring at the princess as if they'd never seen her before—Simeon and Anna included.

"You're new here?" the princess asked Mariel in a sweet bell-like tone. At Mariel's dazed nod, the princess gave a merry laugh and patted a cushion across from her. "I know, darling, I know. Come! I'll show you around this glorious city." Then, to Simeon and Anna, she added, "Follow us, and my servants will attend you. Now come!"

As if she were lost in a dream, Mariel obeyed. She stepped onto the luxurious golden float and sank into a gloriously soft pile of cushions. At a word from the princess, Baby started forward, and the vehicle shuddered as it followed the beast. Simeon and Anna fell into the procession behind the princess, and servants were already draping them with gold scarves and ornaments. Two laughing servant girls busily braided Simeon's creamy mane with gold ribbons.

The princess took off her own crown, which was made of

delicate strands of gold and trailing strings of gold charms, and placed it on Mariel's head. "There you are, dear. Now you don't look so out of place."

Mariel reached up to touch the costly crown in awe that the princess would give her such a gift. It hadn't occurred to Mariel that her lack of gold jewelry and raiment would distinguish her as an outsider. "I'll…I'll give it back before we leave," she said in a voice that wasn't quite her own.

The princess laughed. "Oh, no, darling, that one's yours. I have a great many more." Plucking a silk scarf from a pile of gold cloth beside her, she let it slide into Mariel's hands with a hissing whisper. Mariel was keenly aware of its cool finish, the way the light glimmered with a soft glow around its smooth surface and, as Mariel wound it around her wrists in utter rapture, how it felt as feathery as a cloud against her skin.

Mariel tore her gaze from it and opened her mouth to thank the princess—and screamed instead. She lurched sideways. "Snake!"

It was coiled amongst another pile of gold material and glaring at her, flicking its black tongue. The princess laughed at Mariel's terror. "Now, now, dear, don't be alarmed. I keep these for pets." She held out her hand to the snake, which seemed to Mariel like a golden adder, and the creature willingly wound itself around her long shapely arm and poked his head over her shoulder, rudely flicking its tongue at Mariel again. The princess idly stroked its flat head with graceful fingertips. "See? Gentle as a kitten."

The adder didn't seem very gentle to Mariel at all, but she said nothing. It was a bad idea to argue with a princess one had just met—and even if it wasn't, Mariel had no desire to cross her whatsoever. But for Mariel, the spell was partially broken. Too many memories of the horror she, Anna and Simeon had narrowly escaped were prevalent in her mind.

"So," Mariel began casually, tearing her eyes away from the snake's evil stare, "your city is very beautiful."

The princess gave another lilting laugh. "Isn't it? Its prosperity has made it as beautiful as it is."

Mariel looked out over the throngs of gold-bedecked creatures parting before them. They certainly looked prosperous. "I haven't seen another city like it, er, in all the Menagerie," she finished hastily.

"We're by far the most advanced," replied the princess archly. Mariel glanced back at her in surprise. It was a bold thing to say, and obviously the princess meant it. But pride seemed so much a part of her normal personality that, coming from her, it wasn't unnatural. "The other cities are still restrained in their thinking by what they refer to as 'traditional values'. Ridiculously archaic," and she tossed her hair disdainfully.

Mariel could hardly believe her ears. This golden princess, all beauty and charm, was one of her enemies. And Mariel realized that if she knew about Mariel's mission, she might try to stop her. As if sensing her thoughts, the adder hissed at the girl from his perch on the princess' shoulder.

"Here's a perfect example of what I'm talking about," the princess interrupted Mariel's tense thoughts. She waved a hand at a huge coliseum glimmering and gold in the sunlight. A hundred steps poured from the entrance, and outside of it, the strangest drama was taking place. A large rat, draped in a black judge's robe accented with gold, was descending the glittering steps with a large book in his hand. Mariel watched him pad all the way down and unceremoniously drop the book in the dirt, dust off his paws, and march back up the steps, well satisfied with himself. He disappeared in the far left door.

Mariel craned her neck and studied the book as the beast pulled their float past the gleaming coliseum. "'The Golden Rule'?"

The princess nodded. "Or so it says. But we've been much more prosperous since we've gotten rid of it…however temporarily," she added in annoyance, glowering at a small mouse that poked its head out of the right-hand door. He peered around, then hustled down the steps, nearly tripping over the hem of his black judge's robe in his haste. He gathered the huge book reverently in his paws before hurrying back inside, teetering under the weight of his burden.

Puzzled, Mariel looked back at the princess, who was shaking her head. "What is the Golden Rule?"

"Just a lot of outdated philosophies that no longer apply to modern society," replied the princess flippantly, stroking her snake. "The City of Gold wouldn't be what it is today if someone hadn't dared defy that book, which held us back from our full potential for far too long. We're still in the process of breaking free. Eventually, we will," she added, a confident smile curving her red lips as the rat appeared again, bearing the ungainly volume down the steps. The seven-headed beast carried them steadily past, and the princess seemed to relax again. Her attitude radiated a sort of triumph. "Actually, we should burn it. It came from that old madman and it deserves to go up in smoke."

"Old madman?" Mariel wondered in simple curiosity.

"Yes. Some call him the Zookeeper."

Mariel suddenly choked. "Oh…him?"

The princess' sharp gaze pinned Mariel, and every trace of hospitality vanished. "Yes, him. Do you know him?"

"I, I…well…" Mariel cast a nervous glance at the large number of menservants trailing behind them, belatedly noticing the curved scimitars tucked in their golden sashes. Simeon and Anna were in their midst, looking uncomfortable in their strange golden adornments.

The princess rose off her cushions with the slow menace of

a rattlesnake. Her blazing golden-brown eyes glared at Mariel. "You utter *fool*!" she hissed vehemently, reaching a hand to her shoulder. Her slender fingers curved around the golden adder's neck, and it writhed in her grasp as she drew it away from her body. "How *dare* you come into *my* city and try to undermine everything…everything!" She was quivering with rage. Mariel sat paralyzed under her tirade, shocked at the sudden change in the amiable princess. The adder curled convulsively, and the princess drew her hand back. "Traitor! Do you know what you could have done? Now you will die!"

Mariel sprang away at the last instant and dodged aside just as the princess threw the adder. It landed on a slippery silk cushion and slid out of the float altogether. There was a slight bump in their smooth ride as one of the wheels rolled over it. Furious, the princess reached beneath a golden pillow and lurched to her feet, clutching a golden dagger. Her purple dress billowed about her in the breeze, and with her curly golden hair framing her face like a lion's mane and her white teeth bared between snarling blood-red lips, she resembled some enraged goddess of death.

Mariel scrambled backwards and pressed her back against a post. The princess advanced on the girl, so beautiful and terrible and deadly in her wrath, the golden knife gleaming murderously. Just as the princess lunged, Mariel gripped the post and swung sideways to the ground, and the knife sliced into her forearm. She pulled free of the carriage with a gasp and took off at a run, blood already trickling over her skin. Mariel scrambled to the front of the float. Something slammed into her stomach and knocked her backwards.

Whirling, Mariel let out a gasp of fright when she found herself face to face with the seven-headed horned beast.

Baring its yellow fangs, the beast drew back one of its ugly heads to gore her. With a cry Mariel dodged aside. The beast lurched after her and bellowed, restrained by its golden harness and the float it pulled. The canopy shuddered violently and the princess grabbed onto a pole to keep from falling off.

Mariel hastily recovered, whirled, and ran in the opposite direction. Simeon and Anna bucked the ranks of servants as Mariel raced past. An enraged shriek burst from the princess, who poked her head through the gold curtains and aimed her knife at the fleeing girl.

"After her, you fools! Kill her!"

CHAPTER
FOURTEEN

Mariel heard the metal rasp of several drawn scimitars and fear rocketed through her. With a whole contingent of armed soldiers in hot pursuit, the terrified girl raced past the gold coliseum, where the black-robed mouse was again retrieving the book—seemingly oblivious to the chase happening right in front of him—and hurrying up the one hundred steps with it.

A wild peal of bells from the tower in the square shattered the air. Random blasts from trumpets followed. Alarms were being sounded throughout the City of Gold, and Mariel ignored them all as she ran for her life. If Green Valley High had a track team, Mariel would have been on it. She loved running, and was fleet-footed. But so, seemingly, were her enemies, and Mariel's progress was hampered as she dashed and twisted through crowds of puzzled animals choking the path. She was just an ordinary girl to them, and they paid her no mind. But they parted hastily before the princess' minions.

Those minions were closing the distance, fast.

Suddenly, Mariel shoved past a kangaroo and dashed down a side alley, desperately hoping she'd slipped away from the crowd unnoticed. She risked one glance over her shoulder and found the entire golden army of scimitar-brandishing men pouring into the alley behind her. Cold terror coursed down her spine as she ran through the cluttered passageway, hopping over empty wine barrels with the ease of a hurdler and leaving overturned stacks of gold crates in her wake, thinking madly for some way to elude the pursuing squad of professional killers.

Overturned crates weren't going to do it, she saw in dismay. The soldiers leapt over the obstacles like Olympic hurdlers.

The alley opened into another crowded street, and Mariel darted onto that road and kept on running. Flower, jewelry and cloth vendors were giving away their golden wares, and the bedecked shoppers stared disdainfully at the girl racing past before they willingly stepped aside for the soldiers. One vendor, a gold turban-wearing monkey, was standing obliviously in the pathway and squinting up at the sun. Mariel nearly ran him over.

The monkey leapt aside with a cry. "Ai! Infidel!" he screeched, shaking his fist at her as Mariel recovered and raced on without so much as an apology.

At the word "infidel," several turban-headed monkey heads poked out from behind their booths, staring at the girl as she whizzed passed them.

"A diversion!" one monkey whispered to another, shoving a crate of silk scarves against the wall. "Let's do this now. Alert the others."

Mariel ignored them all, breathless with fear. She rounded a bend in the path and skidded wildly to a halt, staring in horror. A mirror golden army was headed straight for her.

"There she is!" the captain shouted, drawing his scimitar. Mariel saw his platoon doing likewise before she scrambled backwards and swallowed down a cry. In one last desperate bid for her life, Mariel swerved sideways and ran into another alley. At the end there was a gold brick wall with a sign bearing a royal gold crest with the symbol of the princess' seven-headed beast nailed to it: *Do Not Enter.* Mariel entered with all speed and found her way almost immediately blocked by another brick wall.

Mariel slapped her hands against the bricks in pure frustration. "No, not this!" Desperately she looked over her shoulder, hearing the pounding of a hundred feet behind her, the princess' orders for her death ringing in her head. Her wild eyes rushed back to the wall and judged the possibility of scaling it. But it had no cracks to use for handholds and it rose easily twenty feet high. There was a darkened doorway to her left, out of which a faintly rotten smell drifted, and Mariel couldn't see anything inside of it.

The pounding of feet drew ever closer, drowning out her own heartbeat. Mariel ducked into the darkened doorway and found it full of metal dumpsters, all stinking terribly, and there were no exits. She dove between a few of the nearest ones and, keeping her head low, she moved through the maze of dumpsters towards the back of the room.

The whole time, Mariel knew she was doomed. There was

no way out of this garbage room. Any second, the whole golden army would swarm inside and turn the place upside down until they found her. Nevertheless, Mariel hunkered down between the cold dumpsters and waited in the death trap, her eyes closed tightly as she tried to ignore her pending fate and the nauseating odor.

She waited for what seemed a very long time. What was taking them so long? Mariel's legs tingled from lack of circulation, and she sat down on the cold cement and pulled her knees close, shivering in the dark. Maybe they were toying with her. Perhaps they were encamped outside, waiting to ambush her when she finally emerged.

But why? Why not take her now while she was trapped?

Mariel expelled a shuddering breath and opened her eyes a little. Her vision adjusted for the lack of light, and she noticed now a narrow shaft in the ceiling at one end of the room. Gathering her feet beneath her, the girl rose unsteadily and peeked apprehensively over the dumpster at the lighted doorway. No soldiers.

Frowning, Mariel crouched down and shuffled like a turtle towards the shaft. When she reached it, she shoved aside the heavy dumpster situated just beneath it and peered upwards, wondering where that shaft led. It was a perfectly smooth tube, so climbing it would be a problem, Mariel realized. Chewing her lip, she decided to try it anyway.

She was just scrambling precariously atop one edge of the dumpster when a loud metallic bang above her almost stopped her heart. Something heavy scraped across the opening, shooting down a beam of blinding white light. Mariel barely dove out of the way in time before something came hurtling down the shaft and landed with a soft thud on the cement floor. The stone lid scraped back into place, cutting off the light. And everything was quiet.

Mariel remained frozen, counting her skittering heartbeats. An eternity later, the girl slowly rose from her cramped position on the floor, her hand braced on the side of a dumpster. She despaired now of using the shaft as an avenue of escape; it was covered by something heavy. She had to think of something else—something drastic like perhaps hiding amid the garbage, even though she had no way of knowing where the trash was deposited around here. She had no aspirations to be compacted into a neat cube before being tossed into a landfill.

Scowling, Mariel decided to check the walls one last time for any possible doors. As she moved forward, she nearly tripped on something soft and stiff, and she backed up hastily and studied the thing in the dim light. Whatever had fallen from the shaft was still there on the floor, and Mariel moved her body—and her shadow—aside so she could see it a little better.

At once she gave a gasp of horror and stumbled back against a dumpster with a dull echoing clatter. The faint illumination revealed a dead puppy lying on the cement.

"Oh my God!"

Clamping a hand firmly over her mouth, Mariel fought the overwhelming urge to throw up and cry. Her gaze riveted on the little creature. He was fully formed, but pink and hairless and covered in some kind of slick membrane, as if he'd been stillborn. Pressing her back against the cold metal side of a dumpster, Mariel inched away from the awful sight. There was another loud metal scraping above her, and from the shaft of light something else dropped. Mariel made the mistake of looking; it was a stillborn deer fawn.

By the time the light vanished again, Mariel was an emotional mess. She hid her face in her hands and sat down on the cold floor, not moving, while the shaft opened and closed periodically, depositing various stillborn creatures: a horse foal…six piglets...a chinchilla...three rabbits...a sprawling long-legged giraffe...a kangaroo joey...twin polar bear cubs. All of them dead.

Mariel plugged her ears against the awful sounds and refused to watch the growing pile of dead baby animals. Suddenly, her eyes shot open, and a wild terror gripped her. She had to get out of there! Going out the door wasn't an option; the soldiers would be waiting for her. She'd have to risk the garbage's destination, she decided, bracing her hands on the cold metal lip of a dumpster in preparation to climb in.

At once she muffled a scream and stopped, her wide blue eyes drifting over the awful scene. Each and every one of the dumpsters was piled high with the corpses of dead baby animals.

Her senses reeling, Mariel sank to the ground and hugged her knees to her chest, biting her lip and trying not to breathe. She knew now that the rotten odor was not of garbage at all, but of decomposing flesh. She suppressed a soft whimper and shut down her senses.

A moment later, she was startled when the heavy rasp of stone against metal came from the wall, not the lighted shaft. A hidden door opened in the wall, sending a broad swath of white light into the garbage room.

Mariel roused herself immediately and shrank into the shadows as two ugly yellow-eyed hyenas padded into the room, laughing hoarsely about something.

"Junca can eat all za baby rats she wants, 'long as she leaves my mice alone," chortled one spotted hyena in a strangely high-pitched tone.

"Wait, Draco, clarify ziss. Large mice er small mice?" asked his companion.

"Depends on 'ow big za chunks are," slobbered Draco, swiping a tongue noisily over his chops.

Both broke up in coarse laughter. Mariel scowled. She saw no humor in the conversation, and she very much hoped they weren't going to *eat* anything while she was there. She didn't dare poke her head out to see where they were or what they were doing.

"Clumsy oafs!" grouched Draco a moment later. "Will ya lookit ziss, Kaeda? Za night shift iz full 'a lazy slackers. Zay didn't even push za dumpster under za shaft."

Kaeda chuckled. "Ah, but zat means we git to tell za bosses."

Mariel could almost hear the grin in Draco's voice. "Mhmm. Za bosses iz fair beasts. Za missus'll appreciate za fresh baby gator tail za night shift usually gits, I'm sure."

Kaeda nodded and sat down to scratch a mangy ear. "'Ey, speaking 'a bosses, Drac, I was zinkin'."

"Ya shouldn't. It's bad fer ya."

"Oh, stop it. I'm tired 'a zem gettin' za lion's share…"

"Zat can't be 'elped; zay're lions."

"Draco!" snapped Kaeda irritably, pausing to bite at his black toes before speaking again. "'M jest sayin'. 'M tired 'a zem takin' perfectly good meat an' usin' it fer beauty products an' stuff to make all za beasts look younger." Mariel remembered the golden princess' perfect complexion and shuddered. "An' zay don't take good inventory upstairs, and if a few choice morsels were to go missin'…"

"Mmm." Draco was grinning again. "Well let's have za look at what we got 'ere…"

Mariel inched her face around the side of her dumpster and saw them busily sorting through baby creatures. "Oh lookit 'ere!" There was a loud slurp. "Rabbits."

"Lemme see!" Kaeda dove over the fawn he was eyeing and stared greedily at something near Draco's paws. "Iz, um, izzat four?"

"Zree, dummy, zree. 'At means one fer ya an' two fer me."

"Why two fer ya?"

"Cuz I saw zem first."

Kaeda snarled, his eyes blazing. "No fair. 'Twas my idea first."

"So?"

"So I git za two rabbits."

Mariel wasn't sure who piled into whom first. Within seconds both hyenas were embroiled in a full-scale war, growling and snapping, tearing at each other tooth and claw as if they were mortal enemies who hadn't been involved in a friendly chat only a moment before. Mariel seized her opportunity and slunk out of the garbage room during the commotion, crouching down and running through the hidden door.

Once inside the hallway, the brilliant light hurt her eyes and made her feel very exposed. There were no shadows to hide in. The white-tiled floor, white ceiling and white walls were so bright that Mariel could hardly tell where one surface ended and another began.

Hesitantly she began to walk down the corridor, glancing over her shoulder once in a while. She wasn't being followed; she could still hear the faint snarling of the hyena fight taking place behind her. The hallway ended abruptly, leaving her the option of turning left or right down identical hallways.

"Oh great, a mouse maze," Mariel muttered to herself, turning left and praying she was making the right decision. Before she had taken three steps, a large ostrich rounded a corner and glared at her.

"You there, hold still!" she snapped.

Mariel froze. The ostrich came close and cast a cursory glance over her, then leaned close and pecked at Mariel's head. The huge bird was relatively gentle, and Mariel realized the ostrich was straightening the crown the golden princess had given her. Knowing everything she knew now, Mariel wanted nothing more than to rip it off.

"You must be new here. You don't look well," the ostrich observed in a harsh matronly tone. "You've never seen stillborns, have you?"

Mariel hesitated, then quickly shook her head.

"The feeling will pass in time," stated the flightless bird brusquely. "Just remember, they're not really alive yet. They're just blobs of tissue. It's always the mother's choice, you know. Now I strongly recommend you go see the bosses about taking the afternoon off. You're new; they'll understand."

Mariel nodded dumbly, and the ostrich marched past and continued on her way down the corridor, leaving the bewildered girl where she stood. All at once Mariel shook herself and hurried down the hall.

Mariel didn't want to later remember anything she saw in that awful place. Pregnant cattle with bulging sides were being herded into one room, and a separate stream of them were being escorted out, thin and without calves by their sides. Mariel could only guess what had happened to the calves. There were other laboratories labeled *Stem Cell Research, Anti-Aging Department,* and *Skin Care.* Another room advertised *Butchery,* and through the window Mariel saw white lab-coated workers busily slicing and packaging choice cuts of meat.

Feeling as if she'd lost her appetite permanently, Mariel walked past stone-faced doctors and nurses—some humanoid, others ferrets and weasels and ostriches in white lab coats. They didn't ask the girl questions as she hurried in one direction after the other until finally she found the front office. She broke into a run past the startled receptionist fox and burst through the doors, into the sunshine.

The golden streets were just as merry as they had been earlier. Streams of wealthy animals swaggered busily past on their own errands. Mariel bounded down the steps and glanced back just once before she joined them, and she saw the sign on the front of the building which announced: *Health Clinic.*

Utterly bewildered by the atrocities she'd witnessed, Mariel walked down the road in a daze. When she awoke from her stupor, she was hopelessly lost. She turned in a circle, trying to get her bearings in an unfamiliar city.

Suddenly Simeon and Anna were beside her, their strong, warm bodies pressed protectively on either side of her.

Mariel gasped. "Boy, am I glad to see you…"

"Likewise," clipped Simeon. "Let's get out of here."

The horse and the llama led Mariel quickly down the street, and Mariel saw the twin golden spires gleaming in all their wondrous glory. The city gate wasn't far away; evidently she wasn't as lost as she'd thought. The company hurried through the crowd of gold-bedecked animals while Simeon and Anna's ears twitched, constantly alert for trouble.

Mariel felt Anna stiffen. "We're being followed."

"Keep walking," ordered Simeon.

Mariel hid herself against him as much as she dared. The suspense was killing her. A moment later, she risked a glance over her shoulder and met the eyes of the captain.

"You!" he shouted, drawing his scimitar. "It's the girl! After her!"

The company instantly broke into a run. Mariel whimpered softly, trying to ignore her weariness and letting Simeon shove their way through the masses. The gate was getting closer as Simeon and Anna galloped beside Mariel with the soldiers pounding close behind.

Suddenly a brown goat ahead of the company let out a bleat of alarm and shied wildly. Every head in the crowd jerked upwards and found a vendor's cart careening through the air, spilling golden apples in its flight. It smashed into the side of one of the golden towers.

Shrill screams and pandemonium broke out, and Simeon was forced to slow his progress. Anna kept a wary eye on the tower above them, which was spilling debris. It looked structurally unstable, now, and that worried the llama.

Mariel let out a sharp gasp. "The princess…"

Anna turned slightly and saw the enraged princess goading the stubborn seven-headed beast onwards with her whip, now that she'd caught sight of Mariel. "After them, after them!"

Mariel was aghast. Even with the princess' beautiful city under attack, vengeance against a follower of the Zookeeper took precedence. A fresh round of screams caused Mariel to look up, and she saw a second cart slam into the other golden tower at the gate, its spire wobbling precariously. Animals were running in every direction. The soldiers, still in formation, doggedly chased Mariel's group. A wild whooping from celebrating monkeys burst from the merchants' quarter.

"Death to the Infidels!" they hollered again and again.

Simeon muscled his way through the masses, but the oncoming stampede slowed them down. The soldiers were catching up. The princess was urging them on, since the beast balked at all her commands—much to her fury. She whipped the beast with a passion.

There was a monstrous groaning creak above them, and a dark shadow blotted out the sun. Mariel's gaze jerked skywards, and she found a huge section of the first tower breaking off as if in slow motion and plummeting to the ground towards them, scattering huge pieces of debris like confetti. They fell around Mariel's company with dangerous thuds.

"Let's go, let's get out of here!" Mariel shouted above the turmoil, watching the enormous spire descending over their heads. Simeon was already clearing aside a herd of wild rams with his broad shoulders, and Mariel and Anna were trailing in his wake, casting frightened glances at the oncoming soldiers. The golden princess let out a long wailing cry of despair. She'd lost her whip. The beast had snapped his harness free and turned on his mistress, and he stood over her, attacking the helpless princess with all seven of his horned heads. The wild cheers from the monkeys rose deafeningly over the chaos.

"Go!" cried Anna, staring up at the falling skyscraper.

"Run!" yelled Mariel desperately, looking back at the army still chasing after them.

Simeon, Anna and Mariel raced ahead of the tower a second before it came down with a mighty crash, raising a colossal gray-brown cloud of dust and crushing unfortunate animals beneath it. Mariel had time for one glance upward before a large gold chunk of the building slammed into her and pinned her to the ground.

CHAPTER
FIFTEEN

Mariel cried out in pain and surprise as she was thrown to the ground, staring up at the gray sky with a large chunk of gold debris crushing her ribs. Smoke from the explosion stung her eyes. They teared up, and suddenly Mariel couldn't see.

Pinned down and blind, Mariel panicked. "Simeon!" she cried, her voice a pathetic whisper.

"Hold still." Simeon's strong muzzle shoved away the gold, and Mariel sucked in a painful gulp of air. Then she heard the horse lie down with a soft *whump* beside her. Smaller llama teeth gripped the back of Mariel's shirt and dragged her onto Simeon's broad back, and Mariel rolled over and secured her arms around Simeon's neck.

"Hold on!" warned Simeon, lurching to his hooves and lumbering off at a gallop. In the dark, Mariel heard the soft *plicka-plicka-plicka* of Anna's little hooves as she doggedly kept up with the mighty workhorse.

Mariel's eyes watered. Slowly she blinked away the dust from her vision, and the world came into reluctant focus. She glanced over her shoulder at the City of Gold and saw one broken tower still standing beside the one which had already collapsed, the once-proud monument now a pile of smoking rubble. There was a low groan from the other tower, as if it were tired of standing; and it too imploded in a plume of gold dust and black smoke. Panicked animals were running everywhere like ants around a disturbed anthill.

A group of gold-clad soldiers, their scimitars glittering in the sun, broke from the gates and came to a disheartened halt when they saw Simeon and Anna disappearing with their quarry over the distant hills.

"Good Zookeeper," Anna exclaimed as she ran. "Their city was being attacked and falling apart around their ears, and still they were determined to pursue us!"

Mariel moaned, holding tightly to Simeon's mane. The jolting of the workhorse's huge hooves made her bruised ribs throb with every jarring step, and her pale face was pinched with pain. At that moment, a ball of gray-white feathers hurtled out of the sky, landing with great precision on the crest of Simeon's neck. All three companions were startled, especially Simeon, who whipped his huge head to one side and rolled his

155

white-rimmed eyes in an attempt to see his uninvited passenger. The bird lost his balance and nearly fell off.

"Simeon, jeez, chill out!" squawked the seagull, flapping his wings. "I just executed the perfect landing while you were at full gallop and-"

"Marcus!" Anna and Simeon exclaimed at the same time. Simeon automatically slowed to a loping trot.

"Yes, it's me. No, Simeon, pick up the pace! We haven't got much time. Mike sent me to find you and tell you-"

"Who's Mike?" Anna interrupted. Mariel simply sat there, watching dully, and she gave a soft groan as Simeon quickened his smooth gait to a rocking canter. Marcus flapped his wings occasionally to maintain his precarious perch.

"Never mind that!" shouted the bird above the wind. "Just go straight and take a left into the valley. They're all waiting for you!"

He didn't bother to say more. Mariel's mind was whirling with questions, but the pain in her ribs eclipsed everything else. Marcus twisted his head back and gazed at her with some concern.

"You're hurt," he observed.

"You would be too," Mariel gritted out between clenched teeth, "if you had a building fall on top of you."

Fluffing his feathers, Marcus left it at that, and Simeon galloped on with Anna bouncing along behind them. After what Mariel guessed was a couple of miles, they reached a fork in the road, and they veered left as per Marcus' instructions. The wide golden road seemed to go on and on, and though it was in perfect condition, Mariel was not. She closed her eyes and leaned over Simeon's neck, enduring the ride and praying the torture would end soon.

It didn't. After several miles of racing along the road, Marcus said something to Simeon that Mariel didn't quite understand in her state of semi-delirium. The next thing the injured girl knew, they were off the path and cantering over rough ground, following a narrow dirt trail through overgrown golden fields and thorns and brambles.

The pain in Mariel's ribs increased dramatically as Simeon plodded tirelessly on through the endless landscape. Just when she thought she couldn't take any more, Simeon was confronted by a sandy ridge and climbed it at a strained gallop. Mariel whimpered in pain; every step sent bolts of agony through her whole body and stole her breath away.

"We're almost there," soothed a worried Marcus, looking at her with unblinking black eyes.

As soon as Simeon topped the ridge and came to a halt with Anna beside him, Mariel opened her eyes and saw that Marcus wasn't exaggerating. Below them a large green valley opened up like a verdant bowl in the desert. Beside a crystalline spring, a great encampment was going up. Tents were being pegged and small campfires were scattered here and there. Animals were bustling about, the sharpening of iron and the ring of hammers could be heard in the afternoon silence, and Mariel could smell delicious things cooking.

Mariel's hands tightened on Simeon's creamy mane as he descended the ridge, joining with a stream of animals flowing into the valley from every direction. Mariel looked about her in amazement, ignoring her growing discomfort. Noble stags flanked them on their right side, along with rugged mustangs and regal, unhurried moose. On the other side came wildcats: lynxes and cougars and bobcats and leopards. Standing out among them was a pure black panther, moving like a day shadow. She looked up at Mariel with startling emerald eyes and smiled.

Mariel was in too much pain to do more than grimace in return. The panther loped ahead of the pack and vanished in the crowd. Marcus glanced at Mariel, then suddenly flapped off and winged his way swiftly downward into the heart of the valley. Trying to distract herself from her sore ribcage, Mariel let her gaze wander idly over lumbering grizzly bears and enormous buffalo shambling down the sides of the valley while red foxes and striped badgers scampered almost underhoof. Elephants thundered eagerly downwards, trumpeting and flapping their huge ears.

"Welcome," a deep voice greeted them. Looking ahead of them, Mariel found a splendid man dressed in a white tunic and gold armor, astride a horse that was red as fire. Mariel couldn't help gaping as she took in the sight. He had blonde hair and intense blue eyes. They were the eyes of a warrior, yet there was a kindness in them that surpassed Mariel's understanding. Emblazoned on his shield was the symbol of a flaming dove, similar to a Phoenix.

His bold presence was terrifying. On Simeon's back, Mariel trembled.

Simeon bowed his head low. "Thank you, Mike. It's good to have you here in this hour."

"This hour is why I have come," responded Mike, his blue eyes shifting to Mariel. Mariel froze, simultaneously frightened and warmed from the inside out. Then, to the girl's great confusion, Mike bowed his head to her. "You are the Chosen One. It is for the completion of your quest that I have come."

"Er...thank you," Mariel faltered, nodding her head in return and not daring to meet his eyes after that.

At that moment, the sound of cantering hooves approaching made Mariel turn her head. Another rider, a smiling dark-haired gentleman in a cream-colored polo shirt and navy slacks, galloped up to them on a magnificent palomino stallion. Marcus was settled on the fellow's shoulder.

"Mike!" called the rider, coming to a halt before them while the palomino tossed his great head. The man's gray-eyed glance flicked to the girl, then back to Mike. "I hear she's injured." Marcus fluffed his feathers and tried to look humble. "So leave her to me for awhile, but get the council of war started. Already leaders are gathering near your tent."

Mike chuckled, his intense blue eyes meeting Mariel's once more before he wheeled his fiery stallion about. "Come when you can, Simeon." Then he cantered away.

The other rider was already off his horse and looking up at Mariel. "Does it hurt?" he asked gently.

Biting her lip, Mariel nodded. Simeon spoke up for her. "A large chunk of a collapsing building fell on her ribcage, Ralph."

"Oh," returned Ralph sympathetically, gazing up at Mariel, "I'm sorry to hear that. But I can heal you. Come here, child." And he held open his arms to her.

Mariel hesitated, then slid sideways from Simeon's back into Ralph's waiting arms. He held her as gently as if she were a baby, shifting her so that one arm was around her shoulders and the other was beneath her knees. Then, in his warm, deep voice, he sang to her in a soothing language Mariel couldn't understand.

Mariel relaxed immediately and rested her head against his shoulder with a tired mumble. His singing was stealing her pain away. Ralph carried her to a white pavilion, where sunlight streamed in uninhibited and the soft breeze fluttered through the open corners between the white wall panels, and laid her down on an extraordinarily soft bed. He covered her with a navy blanket that caught the sun's rays and kept the girl warm. Mariel sank gratefully into the pillow and was asleep within moments.

The next thing she knew, Anna was gently nuzzling her cheek. "Wake up, little one. We're waiting for you."

Stretching and yawning, Mariel climbed out of bed and followed the llama into the night. She felt completely healed. It was dark already, and stars twinkled down at them from a navy sky. Statues of gold lions stood silent witness to Mariel and Anna's passage. Campfires dotted orange over the entire valley and animals were clustered around them; Mariel could see their silhouettes. From the nearer fires, glowing yellow and green eyes watched her with interest as she passed.

Anna led her to a large bonfire, where a great number of dignified-looking animals were arranged in a circle around the blaze and murmuring to each other. Ralph waved at her, and Mariel smiled gratefully at him. Mike sat on a boulder at the council's head, bronzed in the firelight like a legendary warrior. Mariel could hardly take her eyes from him. Simeon stood beside him, looking somehow more regal than Mariel had ever seen him, his ancient gray head held high. The black panther Mariel had noticed on their way into the valley was sitting quietly near three spotted leopards, her tail curled around her and resting atop her forepaws. Mariel fancied that the enigmatic cat bore a knowing expression in those strange green eyes.

The llama gently nudged Mariel in the back, prodding her into the ring of creatures. A great hush fell over them. Mike raised a hand towards her. "Behold," he said to the gathering, "the Chosen One."

The silence was one of reverent awe. One by one, the animals bowed their heads to her. Mariel shifted uncertainly and bowed in return, then shoved her hands in her pockets and took a step backwards—right into Anna, who was preventing her from leaving.

"Does she have it?" wondered one of the badgers.

Before Mariel could ask what "it" was, the black panther with the emerald eyes spoke up. "She does."

"How do you know?" pressed a hunting falcon, flapping his great wings and giving Mariel a rather unnerving sharp stare.

At that, the panther rose from her place and paced around the roaring fire like the huntress she was, her bold gaze drifting over the company. "Because I have followed them," she responded. "Simeon the Noble and Anna the Wise have brought the Chosen One far—indeed almost since she entered the Menagerie itself."

This caused another outbreak of speculative murmurs. Anna and Simeon seemed as interested and puzzled as Mariel felt.

Mike silenced them with a raised hand. "Speak, Adelle."

With a placid feline smile, Adelle prowled around the fire. "The wolves have been restless of late, and I tracked their movements more carefully. A few spies from the Other Side howled news that I was able to translate. The wolf language is difficult, but I heard them say that the Messenger Gabe had gone out and brought the Chosen One to see the Zookeeper, and that it put their plans in jeopardy."

Another buzz broke out around the circle, and Mike again quieted them and bid the panther to continue. Mariel watched Adelle pace, awed by the feline grace radiating from her while orange and yellow firelight played off her shiny black fur.

"The leader of the wolves was most displeased by the news," Adelle went on to her captive audience. "He immediately sent spies to the cities around the Menagerie, and then he himself went to The Bridge to find out if it was true and to stop her, if indeed it was. He bribed the vultures with a few pounds of red meat and found out, through them, that a girl had been spotted walking in the wasteland between the Other Side and the Bridge. That was all he needed to know, and he scattered the pack along the golden road to intercept her. I am a swift cat," she said matter-of-factly, "but I had my paws full trying to keep up with them. Their anger lent them swiftness and dangerous determination. That they would kill her, whether she was the Chosen One or not, I was utterly certain, and I set out to prevent it."

Mariel shuddered as Adelle revealed her death sentence, and she shifted against Anna's woolly fur for comfort. The cat spared her an indifferent glance before going on. "I lost the wolves for a short time, much to my dismay, and when they regrouped they were furious. They'd lost her in the city and said she now had two companions, a horse and a llama— Simeon the Noble and Anna the Wise." Mariel, at least, was impressed by the titles the council gave to her seemingly ordinary friends. "I knew they had gone to the barn in the country, and I anticipated that the wolves would attack it. I doubled back and raced through the night to find Elaine and her daughters, Andrea and Ella." The three yellow-eyed leopards smiled and ducked their heads at the mention of their names. "They held off the wolves and saved the rusticated community there from destruction."

"Our sincerest thanks to you," Simeon intoned gravely, bowing his head to them. The three cats smiled shyly in return.

"I was tired from my night run, for I'm not as young as I used to be," Adelle went on, "and I stole a few hours of sleep. I almost regretted it, for when I awoke and picked up the trail, I found that the leader of the wolves had not traveled with his pack, but had gone ahead, and I supposed correctly that they'd laid an ambush by the side of the road in Rainbow Haven. I bounded after them as fast as my paws would carry me and nearly arrived too late. They were already under attack."

The entire circle of animals leaned forward as one, intent on Adelle's story. Even Mike was caught under her spell. "As I arrived, I found Simeon and Anna engaged in battle with two of them," growled Adelle. "Simeon had already killed one. They were holding their own magnificently, but I could tell they were losing the fight. I let out a vicious snarl long before I reached them, and the two surviving wolves slunk swiftly into the forest. I am well known to them." At that, she smiled, but then she glanced sideways at Simeon. "I'm sorry I could not stay and help you," she added soberly, including Anna and Mariel in her gaze. "I know that you were injured, but I needed to catch up with the wolves."

"Had you stayed, there was nothing you could have done for us," replied Simeon.

Adelle twitched her whiskers in disappointment with herself, but she nodded and went on. "I tracked the wolves through the woods, but despite their exhaustion from the battle, my own exhaustion from running for miles on end was catching up with me. I lost them, but not their tracks. I had to rest awhile and pick up the trail later."

She paused, staring down at her claws. Mariel couldn't contain her curiosity. "Did you catch them?"

"No," answered Adelle ruefully. "Unfortunately, revealing my presence rendered me ineffective against the wolves. Wolves are wily as foxes—begging your pardon," she told the red and gray foxes sitting at one edge of the ring, which they acknowledged with good-natured nods. "Once they knew I was there, they tricked me several times in an attempt to throw me off their scent."

"And it worked," remarked Mike thoughtfully.

Adelle lowered her green eyes and nodded. "Too well, I fear. I lost them completely. But I have spied on the wolves a long time, and I have learned to think as the leader thinks. It is my opinion that the wolves are in the Capital already, waiting for the Chosen One's arrival—with reinforcements. They would do anything to prevent her from replacing the Rules of Freedom from supplanting their phony Rules of Free Will with the Rules of Freedom."

A heavy silence fell over the animals. Adelle paced away from the fire and sat down beside the three leopards. A few pairs of eyes looked apprehensively to Mike, who was sitting on the boulder and stroking his chin in deep thought.

Mike straightened and eyed each member of the council. Not many could withstand his bold stare for long, and many a proud gaze was cast down. "When Marcus relayed news of the Chosen One's arrival to me, I sent messengers through the land to gather you, the Faithful, here and begin work on building an army. We have made weapons of war and golden lions. I, too, know the mind of the enemy, and they are aware of restlessness in the Menagerie—and they also know that the Zookeeper would aid those who still serve him. The Zookeeper is benign, but very powerful. Yet even realizing the folly of opposing him, they persist."

The badger held up her paw. "But they shouldn't suspect anything. All we've been doing so far is marching around the walls and holding up signs of protest, which the Zookeeper told us to do."

"Already they've made peaceful protest a dangerous occupation, Jean," pointed out a red fox, twitching his whiskers. "They've done all they can to stop us—as if taking away our rights in the Capital wasn't enough. They know that if you make peaceful revolution impossible, you make violent revolution inevitable. They'll be prepared, trust me."

"I think they want us to fight," put in Elaine, the mother leopard. "They believe that those peaceable by nature will be easy to defeat."

Simeon whickered softly. "Let them go on thinking that."

"If they have already mustered an army," began a grizzly bear near Mariel, "we could find ourselves outnumbered."

"And at a disadvantage, Hunter," returned Mike unhelpfully. "They have seen us coming. Too many vultures are on their side now. We will be going against them on their home turf, as well. The Capital is firmly in their clutches. Nevertheless," he went on, as all the animals sagged at the truth of his words, "let us remember what we came for. Mariel Stone, bring forth the Rules of Freedom."

Every pair of eyes riveted on the girl. Mariel swallowed hard and stepped forward nervously, withdrawing the little worn scroll from her pocket and holding it up in the firelight. To her great amazement, even in the nighttime silence, Mariel felt a wave of courage ripple through the council at the mere sight of it. It was like a beacon of hope, a symbol of liberty. Mariel suddenly felt honored to carry it.

"The Zookeeper has sent her," Mike declared. "He is on our side. The time was appointed by Him, and it is now. Mariel Stone," he said to her, his blue eyes locked with hers, "as residents of the Menagerie, we give you our sincerest thanks that you, who dwell on the Other Side, would take up our cause. From this point forward, you are not alone. Your mission is our mission. We will help you return the Rules of Freedom to its rightful place." A great warmth flooded through Mariel, and she smiled until he continued. "We need to get you inside the Capital so you can replace the scroll."

Mariel shivered. "But…what about the wolves?"

"Leave them to me," answered Mike calmly. "I have a plan."

"Mike and I helped the Zookeeper with the original planning and construction of the Capital," interjected Ralph, his kind gray eyes soothing away some of Mariel's fears. "I'll draw you maps tonight so you'll know your way around once you get inside."

Mariel nodded and sat down beside Ralph. She didn't pay attention to the remainder of the council. There were a few tactical details to discuss beyond Mariel's understanding. Mike divided up the animals into separate regiments, appointing captains among their ranks, but already Mariel was thinking ahead to what tomorrow might hold.

Before she knew it, the council concluded. Mike stood up, tall and fearless, with the flames playing on his gold armor so that he seemed made of fire. "We attack at dawn."

CHAPTER
SIXTEEN

Yawning and rubbing her eyes, a sleepy Mariel slumped on Simeon's back, visions of Ralph's diagrams still running through her mind. The first streaks of dawn were already invading the eastern sky. The tired girl could just make out the faint silhouettes of creatures around her—an entire company of grim-faced animals marching on either side of her, illuminated only by the coming morning. The troops to her left were on foot, hoof and paw, and those who could carried iron spears and swords. Mariel and Simeon rode with the artillery corps, made up of creatures pushing giant golden lions ahead of them. They were escorted by animals bearing torches in their forepaws. The lions glinted faintly, at once both beautiful and deadly.

Leading the crowd was what appeared to Mariel as a blazing pillar of red fire. She leaned low over Simeon's neck, her eyes never leaving the vision. "Is Mike's horse actually flaming?"

A single snort of amusement met her question. One ear flicked towards her. "Possibly. That's West Wind. All the horses of the Zookeeper's highest servants are special. Did you notice Ralph's steed? That palomino stallion is called Southern Sun."

"They're beautiful," Mariel breathed, thinking of Gabe's horse North Star. "But I don't see Southern Sun glowing." Ralph was riding his palomino near the end of the line. He was a healer, not a warrior, and a small force of animals whose sole purpose was to care for the wounded walked with him.

"Southern Sun is special in his own right." Simeon chuckled and turned his muzzle to one side, his dark eye finding Mariel's gaze. "Are you ready for this?"

"No, not really," responded the girl drolly, drawing another half-smile from Simeon. "But neither is anyone else, so I'm in good company."

For a moment the horse looked away and trotted on in silence. Then he veered aside from the streams of marching animals and came to a halt on a shallow ridge, and turning his great head he nuzzled Mariel's knee.

Simeon cleared his throat, and Mariel suddenly realized the great workhorse was on the verge of tears. "You take care of yourself, little one. Follow Mike's instructions, replace the scroll, and get out of there. And if you get in trouble, you just..." He clenched his jaw, and a muscle in the side of his face twitched. "You just call for help, and I'll get to you, somehow."

Mariel's heart warmed and ached at the same time. She leaned down and put her arms around Simeon's neck, his thick mane rough against her cheek. "I'll do my best, Simeon."

"You've never done any less for us."

They remained like that for awhile, each deriving comfort from the other, while the steady flood of creatures loyal to the Zookeeper poured out of the valley and into the plain and the gold lions made slow, steady progress ahead of them. In the dawn's early light, Mariel could see the enormous marble Baroque-style buildings that made up the Capital. The whole city seemed to radiate its once-great history and legacy. In front of the great wall surrounding those ancient pillared domes, the girl noticed a grayish fuzz moving near the ground like a mist over a cemetery.

"Oh," she said in great disappointment, "Mike was right. They're waiting for us."

An opposing force was gathering before the Capital. Mariel recognized the forms of rhinoceroses, wolves, a handful of elephants; hundreds of donkeys, horned goats in seemingly every color and variety, and pale yellow dog-like creatures loping stiffly about: hyenas. Mariel shuddered, remembering some of the nature documentaries she'd watched. Hyenas could be exceedingly cruel. The gold-clad scimitar-wielding foot soldiers Mariel recognized from the City of Gold were scattered throughout the animal ranks.

"We're outnumbered," Mariel breathed.

There was an awkward silence. "Well, we have our advantages too," returned Simeon too quickly. "There's…um, for instance, we have…"

Mariel made a face and bounced a heel lightly against his ribcage. "Come on, Simeon."

The horse coughed. "All right, we're outnumbered."

Mariel sat up again to watch Mike's army advancing on the Capital. Vultures and crows circled overhead in an orange dawn. A distant storm rumbled angrily in the east, obscuring the rising sun, and lightning struck the horizon. The very air was alive with electricity.

Suddenly there was a lone blast from a trumpet, and the defenders of the Capital grew restless, buzzing like bees around a disturbed hive. The single trumpet was joined by a chorus of others until they blared out deafeningly over the plain. A portion of the defenders separated from the main group and advanced to meet the Zookeeper's faithful. They pushed ahead of them large black metal dragons with gaping snouts full of sharp fangs and burning red eyes.

Mariel's breath quickened. The battle for the Menagerie was about to begin.

Simeon turned his head and met her eyes. "Shall we?"

Mariel sat up tall and squared her shoulders. "Wish me luck, Simeon."

"I'll give you something more substantial than luck," answered the horse, lifting his head higher. "The Zookeeper go with you, Mariel."

"And with you, Simeon." Mariel patted his neck.

They moved aside from the rest of the army, letting the other animals go ahead, and fell in behind the group pushing the golden lions onto the battlefield. Mariel slid off Simeon's back and walked beside him, partially hidden from the enemy forces. Hunter, the grizzly bear captain, was in charge, and he growled at his troops.

"Shake a leg, we haven't got all day. Let's get these pieces of junk out there. What'd you all eat for breakfast, iron? Move it!"

Mariel listened with growing amusement to his jargon,

absently stroking Simeon's neck. Suddenly Mike was waving his arm and shouting orders at the grizzly bear, pulling West Wind up so suddenly that the flaming stallion reared and struck fiercely at the air.

"Hunter, stay!" West Wind landed in full gallop, and they streaked across the front lines so swiftly that Mariel thought they'd surely set the ground afire. Mike pulled up short before Adelle, but his blue eyes drifted to Mariel, who peered at him over Simeon's broad back. "Adelle, come in the third wave. Don't charge until we make it to the wall." He spoke to the black panther, but his gaze remained on Mariel, and he gave the girl a nod.

Mariel nodded in response. The line of golden lions ground to a halt as Mike whirled and galloped back to his armies, taking the lead. Mariel's heart hurt as she watched him, fearless and bold, riding his blazing stallion. He was creating a deliberate diversion away from her.

The grizzly swung his massive head around to Mariel. "It's time," he snarled to her.

Mariel gulped and nodded. Before she could think herself out of the idea, she darted forward to one of the lions and crouched down to release a hidden panel in its stomach. Light danced off the shallow surfaces within, roughly carved into a hollow egg-shaped oval. It wasn't very spacious, but plenty large enough to accommodate a girl Mariel's size.

Fear gripped her. It felt like a death trap she was crawling into, and she suddenly questioned Mike's wisdom concerning the whole crazy idea. She didn't know that she should go through with it…

Doubtfully Mariel looked back at Hunter and found his deep brown eyes on her. The time for questions was over. It was Mike's way or no way. Steeling her nerves, Mariel crawled inside the belly of the lion and braced her feet against the lion's throat. Someone closed the panel below her, and her whole world was swallowed up in thick darkness.

Mariel sagged and sat down against the closed panel, frightened. She could hear the sound of her own breathing magnified in the dark, and she couldn't tell the difference between when her eyes were closed and when they blinked open. Her heart hammered in her chest. From somewhere above her, the lion's open mouth provided a little oxygen, but it was still too early for any light to filter into her hiding place. But it did provide Mariel with a fragile connection to the outside world. Distantly she could hear the sound of the animals marching about, orders being shouted out, and the galloping of hooves from the front lines. Among them she knew Simeon had taken his place beside Mike, and she shivered. How she wished she could curl up and cry, or wake up and find that this had all been a dream.

She waited...and waited...and waited. The storm was closer now, and thunder rumbled right through the lion and into Mariel's bones. And then, everything stopped.

For a breathless moment, Mariel wondered if something had gone terribly wrong and Mike's elaborate plan had failed. That concern was immediately shattered. There was a loud whine and a brief flash of red from beyond the lion's mouth. Something collided with the lion and the ground, then exploded. The lion jarred violently and Mariel's head slammed into the unforgiving gold wall. She cried out and put her hand to her temple. Her fingers came away wet with her own blood.

Suddenly Mariel panicked, thumping her fists against the lion. "Let me out, let me out!" she screamed. She fumbled for the latch, but another fiery earthquake shuddered through the lion and Mariel changed her mind. If she climbed out of the lion now, she'd be killed within seconds. But that was the least of her problems. The temperature inside the golden lion was rapidly rising. The gold acted like an oven around her, conducting the heat from the fires and holding it all in the confined space. She tried to keep her skin from coming in contact with the hot metal—which was nearly impossible. Sweat did nothing to ease her discomfort. "Please," she cried out, "I don't want to die in here!"

But her voice was lost in chaos. More dragon's fireballs plummeted around her. Mariel braced her hands and feet against the impact, keeping her injured head away from the lion's sides to avoid hurting it further. Sweat trickled down her back. Warm blood was already matting her hair and there was hardly enough oxygen to sustain her panicked hyperventilating.

Outside Mariel's lion, the battle raged. Mariel knew that Mike's faithful had collided with a wave of beasts defending the Capital, and she could hear a snarling free-for-all with creatures fighting tooth and claw against each other. The black dragons were spitting fireballs which arced over the ferocious skirmish, and the lions were shooting them right back, painting the battlefield orange and red and setting the dry field ablaze with wildfire.

Mariel thought the earthquakes would never stop. She was banged and bruised; there wasn't a part of her that didn't hurt. She was getting weak. The rising sun heated the golden lions further, and Mariel could see the play of reddish flames from the lion's mouth. She was being engulfed in an inferno.

And then, as suddenly as it all began, it stopped. Mariel ceased struggling to listen and heard a stampede of fading hooves moving away from her.

"Retreat! Retreat!" The cries were growing more faint.

Mariel felt like crying. They'd lost...the battle was over...and they'd abandoned her. Miserably she curled up in the hot darkness, damp with sweat and blood and tears, the acrid odors of burnt grass finding their way inside her hiding place. She hardly cared what was going to happen next. She was going to die. Her mind sank into a drugged state of semi-consciousness brought on by the intense heat.

The next thing Mariel knew, there were harsh voices outside the gold lion. A rough jolt startled her into catching her hands against the lion's side, and she hardly dared to breathe.

"They should'a stuck with their marchin' an' their sign-wavin'," came one guttural voice, accompanied by a burst of loud guffaws. "Ya cain't go from sign-wavin' to fightin' with the big dogs. Else you're gonna get whupped!"

Mariel bit her lip against a whimper, hardly daring to breathe. Her enemies were all around her.

"Wal, this is what I call a reg'lar trophy collection. Bring 'em in, boys." Something slapped against the side of Mariel's lion, and fear exploded within her.

There was another violent shudder from the lion, and Mariel gritted her teeth as a painfully jarring trip across the scorched land began. They were pushing and pulling the abandoned lions into the Capital itself. Mariel sniffled and raised her eyes to the one dim source of light coming from the lion's mouth somewhere above her, and she prayed the torture would end soon…and that, when they found her, she'd be granted a swift death.

Seemingly hours later she heard the creaking of giant gates, and the lion's rollers were riding along smooth ground—a welcome relief for the battered girl. The giant gates slammed behind them with an ominous thud. Mariel huddled in the belly of the lion, hugging her knees close. Then she rolled to a stop, and the outside world fell silent.

Mercifully she was no longer in the sun—she could feel that much. The heat began to filter out of the lion in clouds of steam from its snarling mouth. Mariel shivered, as much from fright as the sudden loss of warmth against her sweat-drenched skin.

Suddenly there was a wild cheer from outside the lion. The entire Capital erupted in shouting and celebration. There was laughter and the pounding of hooves as creatures rushed past on the stone streets, and the staccato beat of other hooves told Mariel that some of them were dancing. Nearby came the sound of a loud metallic clang, as if one of the golden lions had toppled onto its side, and a rhythmic striking of a hammer against it echoed the frantic beating of Mariel's heart. And the mob began to chant with each stroke of the hammer:

"The lions are dead! Long live freedom! The lions are dead! Long live freedom!"

Mariel lifted her head, her breathing coming in shallow gasps. They were destroying the lions. They were going to rip apart *her* lion and find her, and nightmarish visions of being seized and dragged through the streets to a French Revolution-style execution flitted before her eyes. She curled up in sheer terror, sobbing.

Why did I ever agree to this? she wondered as the hammers outside collided with solid gold. She shivered and hugged her knees close. *Why didn't I stay home, where it was safe? I've accomplished nothing...I've come all this way, just to die...all for nothing.*

It was the futility of her mission that upset her more than anything. If only she had something, *anything* to die for...

In the midst of her trembling and her sobs, she remembered the face of the Zookeeper, with his Father Christmas beard and his ageless brown eyes, all kindness and benevolence and genuine caring, and sorrow on behalf of the Menagerie—*His* Menagerie. Mariel's tremblings eased and her eyes opened.

"I would die for *you*, Zookeeper," she whispered to the darkness. "At least I will die...doing what you asked of me."

She dropped her head in defeat. It wasn't much comfort, but it was all she had.

At that moment, there was a horrible jolt to Mariel's lion, and she braced her hands against the gold sides. She felt the lion tipping, and the lion—and the girl—were slammed to the ground. Mariel gave a ragged moan of agony. Wretched cackling came from outside, and a wild cacophony of musical instruments burst to life as a hammer began to pound methodically at the head of the lion. Mariel shrank towards the lion's hind legs and huddled there, watching a shallow dent appear in the lion's neck and waiting for the inevitable.

A blast of trumpets broke over the air. And then suddenly there was a shrill scream in the distance, followed by another, and another. Terror swept like wildfire through the celebrating throngs. There was a tremendous crash, followed by an earthquake. Mariel's lion trembled from the pounding of panicked feet and hooves and paws rushing past her.

Everything fell silent. Instinct told Mariel she was alone. She hardly dared trust that instinct, but this might be her only chance. She seized it.

Twisting a small knob on the lion's belly panel with trembling fingers, Mariel banged at it with her fist until it popped free and the exhausted girl tumbled to the ground. The air was freezing cold as it washed over her sweat-drenched clothes, which were plastered against her body. Whimpering softly, Mariel pushed herself up on shaking arms and looked around.

The air was choked with a fog of red-brown dust.

Coughing softly, Mariel clamped a hand over her face and blinked the tears away, wondering what was going on. Through the haze, the thick walls around the Capital had been reduced to piles of rubble, and beyond that, Mariel could see a single flame dashing towards the Capital with a dark throng following it like an approaching thunderstorm.

Mariel narrowed her eyes, recognizing buffalo and bears in the moving mass. She gasped, her eyes darting back to the burning flame leading them. It was Mike! They had returned! And all the Defenders had gone out of the city to meet them, furious and at a disadvantage. One group was scrambling to get the black dragons in place and operating, but they were too late.

Mariel climbed dizzily to her feet, sudden purpose flowing through her. She was alive! Quickly she glanced around and got her bearings. Thanks to the very accurate diagrams Ralph had drawn in the dirt, Mariel knew where she was immediately, and she ran down the deserted golden road. Her destination wasn't much farther now.

The enormous buildings made Mariel feel as small as an ant by comparison. The colonnades of towering pillars rose to the heavens, holding up enormous domes and coliseums and Parthenon-style buildings. Statues of angels, larger than life, looked down on her from the soaring gutters and huge monuments. The city was a marvel of architecture and design; if Mariel weren't in such a hurry, she'd have stopped to gape and take it all in.

But there was no time for that now. She ran as though she had the black dragons on her heels, up one street and down another, until at last she spotted one circular structure made of gray marble. A pair of stone tablets was smashed to pieces before a massive flight of steps, which led to the front doors.

"Finally," breathed Mariel, panting. She padded up to it and took the steps two at a time, but she had to stop and catch her breath halfway up. They'd built a veritable mountain of steps to climb. But at last she made it to the unguarded doors and threw them open, stepping gingerly into the huge dome.

Pale light spilled onto the stone floor, and Mariel's shadow stretched twenty feet ahead of her. The inside was just as large and imposing as the outside. Mariel's tentative footsteps echoed from the stone surfaces, and painted on the ceilings soaring above her were strange depictions of what Mariel guessed was a part of the Menagerie's history, with ancient wise men and various animals in Roman-style togas discussing what Mariel assumed to be matters of political importance. She moved deeper into the circular chamber and froze.

She was being watched by nine huge men.

Then Mariel forced herself to breathe. They were just statues. Nine stone heads mounted on their pillars were carved to show such intense eyes that Mariel thought they truly *were* watching her. They looked like three-dimensional replicas of characters in the paintings above them, and the eyes that seemed to move when Mariel moved were merely an optical illusion.

Mariel's attention drifted to a great stone case in the center of the circle. At once, she gave a soft cry of joy. In the middle of it sat a scroll identical to the Rules of Freedom Mariel carried in her pocket, but it seemed newer and well-preserved. A single shaft of sunlight from a skylight shone down on it.

Mariel's heart beat faster. Forgetting her exhaustion, she hurried forward to complete her mission, her fingers withdrawing the Zookeeper's precious scroll from her jeans' pocket as she trotted across the vast room.

A low snarl stopped her in her tracks. Stepping out from the shadows of the scroll case was the black wolf himself, laughing darkly at her.

"Did you forget about me, missy?" he taunted with an awful smile. A faint shuffle from around the room intruded on Mariel's senses, and whirling she saw motley gray wolves stepping out from behind the stone pillars, leering at her with bared fangs and wicked grins.

Mariel swallowed hard. She'd wandered into a trap. The ring of wolves closed in around her, and Mariel saw her intended death in their murderous, gleaming yellow eyes.

The black wolf gave a low snarl and deliberately licked the scar across his nose—the one Mariel had given him in Rainbow Haven. "I sure didn't forget about you, missy."

CHAPTER
SEVENTEEN

Something happened to Mariel as she gazed into the murderous yellow eyes of the wolf. She knew she was about to die. A part of her steeled for the end, and a strange calm settled over her. Suddenly, she wasn't afraid. When that fear—the fear of death—lost its grip on her, the wolves seemed to shrink. She saw them all as mere dogs. As she stared down the black wolf, his yellow eyes changed. He seemed to know that something was different—something that threatened his superiority.

"I haven't forgotten you, either," said Mariel. Every wolf in the room froze at her bold tone. "Neither has the Zookeeper."

For an instant, a deadly quiet fell over them, as if the wolves had turned to stone. Then the spell broke. The wolves had a startling reaction to the Zookeeper's name. As they snarled and gnashed their fangs, one of them crouched and sprang at her.

Mariel leapt aside and shoved over one of the massive pillars. It slammed onto the wolf and the stone head atop the pedestal shattered. A mad growling erupted from the deceased wolf's furious pack mates, and the ring collapsed on Mariel just as the whole chamber began to shake violently. Monstrous cracks splintered the mighty walls. Stones jarred loose from the ceiling. Mariel lost her balance as the vicious earthquake sent two stone pillars crashing down on the circle of wolves, crushing several of them.

Mariel landed on all fours and looked up at the scroll case, standing before her with the single ray of sunlight gleaming down on it. Mustering her courage, Mariel crawled towards it while shards of rock peppered her skin, stinging her. Suddenly she let out a shrill cry of pain when sharp teeth sank deep into her ankle and dragged her backwards across the smooth cement.

Whipping around, Mariel saw the black wolf glaring at her and biting her ankle right through her sock, blood flowing around the sides of his mouth and soaking into the hem of her jeans. Mad with pain, Mariel kicked his muzzle, determined to make him let go. But he ground his fangs deeper until he struck bone.

Mariel screamed in agony. "Off...off!" She kicked out again, desperately, again and again and again, until she landed a hard blow to his sensitive nose. His grip loosened just enough for Mariel to wrench her leg free. Blood streamed onto the stones as she crawled forward, reaching the scroll case. She seized it with shaking hands and hauled herself upright, clinging to it for dear life as the chamber roiled like a whale in its death throes. The earthquake pitched wolves around, pummeling them with stone debris raining from the ceiling. Loud howls and snarls echoed around the chamber.

With shaking fingers, Mariel made a swipe for the scroll which sat on the small stone pedestal—and missed. The earthquake, combined with her dizziness from pain and loss of blood, made it appear to Mariel's dazed mind as if there were three scrolls. Mariel whimpered as a chunk of falling rock struck her shoulder, and she made a wild grab for the scroll in the middle. Then her fingers closed around solid parchment.

As she replaced the Rules of Free Will with the Rules of Freedom, there was a soft cracking noise. The stone pedestal the scroll rested upon shifted open as if by magic, revealing a golden key within.

Mariel gasped in wonder and took the key. The hidden compartment closed again, and the seam in the rock sealed in a small burst of light as if it had never been there. Mariel slumped forward in exhausted relief, leaning wearily against the scroll case as the chamber around her continued its convulsive bucking. Her mission was complete.

"Not so fast," snarled a wolf, imprisoning her ankle in steel jaws. He yanked her back so suddenly that Mariel lost her grip on the scroll case and slammed hard to the floor, crying out in pain. Mariel clung to the key in her fist as the wolf dragged her backwards and then stopped. The merciless grip on her foot was gone.

Shaking and frightened, Mariel lifted her head a little, and through a mist of tears she saw a shadow fall over her. She froze. Slowly, she raised her head, and found the black wolf glaring down at her, a specter of evil with hell burning in his yellow eyes and blood dripping from his injured nose. The earthquake shuddered to a halt and everything was deathly quiet.

Wounded wolves picked themselves out of the rubble, choking on dust and limping as they formed a glowering circle around the fallen girl. Mariel's wide blue eyes shifted from one snarling muzzle to another.

A dark chuckle brought her gaze back to the leader. "No way out, missy," he growled, grinning. Then he leaned close to murmur in her ear. "I must commend your effort, though. Oh, and thank you for giving me the key to the Menagerie." Chuckling hideously, he watched as Mariel drew the hand holding the golden key close to her stomach. "I'll tell you a little secret. We could never have gotten it without you. For that alone, I must express my gratitude."

Horror sent a chill through Mariel as she realized what she'd done. By replacing the true scroll, she'd released the key to the Menagerie...yet what else could she have done?

With a groan Mariel dropped her head to the cold cement as the answer became clear. Nothing. Her mission was doomed from the start.

The wolf gave a horrible laugh of triumph. "Where is your Zookeeper now, eh?" Mariel closed her eyes and shuddered. Licking his teeth, the black wolf whispered in her ear. "Say goodbye, missy."

CHAPTER
EIGHTEEN

Sharp fangs barely grazed the back of Mariel's neck before they were interrupted by a loud explosion from the front doors. Simeon burst into the chamber, snorting furiously. Mariel's eyes flew open and she cried out when she saw him, but the horse was already in full gallop, bearing down on the ring of wolves. He reared up over Mariel, and with a scream she curled up in a ball and put her arms over her head. There was a tremendous thud as all four of the huge horse's hooves came down beside Mariel, plowing into the ring of wolves and sending them scattering.

Mariel whimpered and crawled away, struggling to ignore the fiery pain searing through her wounded leg. She turned her face away from the wolves and saw a huge, hulking grizzly bear shape block the remaining light from the chamber entrance. Hunter shambled inside and swept his glowering gaze from one end of the room to the other. Mariel whimpered and shrank back—right into the paws of the black wolf.

That galvanized the wolf into action. He fitted his jaws again to Mariel's neck, but before he could close them, a one-ton blur of gray fury slammed into the wolf, knocking them both across the room. Mariel lay curled up in a ball, trying in vain not to listen to the sounds of continued battle around her. Then there was a horrible stomp and a crunch.

Everything in the chamber went dead silent. Slowly, the frightened girl turned her head to look at Simeon.

It was a mistake. The workhorse was standing, panting and blowing steam from his nostrils, over the remains of the black wolf.

With a loud cry, Mariel whipped her head away just as pandemonium broke loose. Infuriated wolves leapt at Simeon to avenge their fallen leader. They swarmed over him, leaping at him, biting his neck, his legs and his flanks; fiercely determined to drag the mighty horse to the ground. Still others attacked Hunter, who swatted them around with his powerful paws like bothersome flies.

Suddenly, a large section of the roof gave way. Bricks fell with a thunderous crash and a gray cloud of plaster rose, setting Mariel to choking. A dark winged creature descended on Mariel, and before she could panic, a pair of enormous clawed talons landed beside her, and the fearsome yellow eyes of a bird of prey glared down at her. Mariel froze. It was the largest bald eagle she'd ever seen. He unfurled his great wingspan protectively over her.

"Stay put, milady!" commanded the huge bird.

Mariel didn't dare disobey.

Mariel was momentarily sheltered, but from her place on the floor she could feel a series of earthquakes that began and ended at intervals, growing increasingly stronger like the approaching footsteps of Godzilla.

"The dragon is coming!" growled Hunter, swatting a wolf aside and lumbering towards Simeon. "Simeon, hold on…" He was immediately engulfed by another vicious wave of wolves, and snarling he grappled with them.

Horror gripped Mariel and she huddled under the eagle's wing. From somewhere in the gray mist came sounds of scuffling and the throaty grunts and whines of fighting beasts, and Mariel picked out Simeon's voice from the chaos. His breathing was becoming more labored, his roars more desperate than angry; and Mariel felt terror on his behalf rising up in her. The earthquake was getting closer.

"Freedom!" gasped Simeon's voice. "Go!"

The huge eagle ducked his head to Mariel's level. "Come on!"

The girl grabbed two fistfuls of white neck feathers and hauled herself aboard Freedom's back. With a mighty heave, Freedom launched the two of them into the air and they soared upward.

Simeon gave a loud cry of pain, and Mariel looked down to see him with his ears pinned and his neck stretched upwards, straining to stay on his hooves while the wolfpack was bent on pulling him down. He was sleek with sweat, his strength fading, and for a moment his white-rimmed eyes met Mariel's.

"Simeon!" she screamed to him as the eagle carried her away. "Don't!"

Simeon locked his desperate gaze with hers, and she put out a hand to him, her heart crying to help him. And then his hooves slipped on the bloody cement. The horse went down hard and disappeared beneath the roiling pack, and Mariel screamed his name again as they hurtled out of the chamber and into the stormy skies.

Choking, Mariel fought to hold onto Freedom. She wanted nothing more than to bury her face in his feathers and sob, but she had to concentrate to keep her balance and the swirling heights made her stomach queasy.

Freedom cast a yellow eye back at her. "Don't look down!" he warned.

But it was too late. Mariel had already looked, and she couldn't tear her gaze away from the awful sight. Inside the Capital, beneath a cloud of smoke and flame, Mike's gallant force was clashing fiercely with all the creatures of the Menagerie. Dead animals were strewn through the city, and the streets ran red with blood.

Rising above the tallest of the skyscrapers was a dark red dragon. He moved in a serpentine fashion, lithe and deadly; breathing great blasts of fire at the Zookeeper's army. One stream of flames reduced a line of badgers to ash, and another left a blackened crater where a company of foxes had been. Nothing withstood the power of his wrath—not even Mike, who rode out to meet him with drawn sword, and his valiant flaming stallion twisted and dodged the fires erupting from the huge serpent's mouth.

"Oh, no…they're all going to die…" Mariel couldn't bear to watch anymore. She put her face in Freedom's feathers.

Freedom flapped his mighty wings, and Mariel could feel

him straining forward to fly faster. "Have to reach...Zookeeper," gasped the valiant bird. "He's...our only hope..."

Mariel lapsed into a semiconscious state. The exhausted girl's ankle was pulsing with pain. Her one thought was to hang on to Freedom, no matter what. Freedom soared higher, and Mariel could see the Menagerie speeding by through the shifting screen of clouds; and on the horizon was the brilliant blue of distant mountains on the Other Side. It was then that she realized how dull and dreary a place the Menagerie really was. Having spent so much time in it, she'd almost forgotten how vibrant colors were supposed to be.

The twisting, turning path Mariel had toiled through for days was, by the swiftness of Freedom's wing and a more direct route through the skies, reduced to mere hours. But each hour seemed an eternity to the poor girl, who rested her forehead against the mighty eagle's back and tried not to think of her friends and the Zookeeper's army in jeopardy. But riding on a huge bird through the air gave her nothing else to think about instead, and all she could see in her mind's eye was Simeon being pulled to the ground by a pack of angry wolves. Mariel bit her lip, choking back a sob, closed her eyes and endured the trip.

Freedom's cry of "Hold on!" woke her up. Her head lurched upright and she looked around, startled, as the great eagle tucked his wings and descended at a steep angle that made Mariel's stomach quiver. The black gate grew larger as Freedom neared it, and on the Other Side, the Zookeeper and Gabe were already mounted and waiting for them. Their white horses were prancing with impatience.

"Hang on, Mariel!" shouted Freedom as they streaked toward the huge gate. He flared his wings at the last moment and brought Mariel in for a surprisingly gentle landing. She slid gingerly off the feathered back, holding her wounded ankle off the ground with a grimace. Her knees were shaky from the long flight, and she nearly toppled sideways as she tried to balance on one foot.

Desperately, she looked up at the lock. It was easily five feet out of her reach. "Freedom... I... I can't..."

"You have to!" cried the eagle, fluttering his wings nervously before tucking them firmly against his back. "I can't do it for you."

Mariel gripped two bars and pulled her body up, but when her injured ankle touched the hard iron, it sent a sharp jolt of pain through her leg. With a cry, Mariel let go.

"Freedom," she cried frantically, "I can't do this."

The huge eagle fluffed his feathers, making himself look even larger. "Yes, you can! Think of the Zookeeper. Think of—" then he had an absolute inspiration. "Think of Simeon!"

Mariel bit her lip. The horse had died for her, just to see her reach this gate safely with that key. She grabbed the bars and pulled herself up, whimpering at the pain, but climbing steadily upwards until, at last, she was level with the lock. She wrapped her feet tightly around one of the bars—which hurt even worse—and crammed the key into the lock. She turned it. It clicked.

The gate sprung open with the girl still clinging miserably to it, and she heard the thunder of hooves from behind it. She barely glanced sideways in time to see the two white horses blazing past and disappearing over the horizon. And behind them came the sunlight, bursting inside the Menagerie and filling the whole world around them with brilliant color. The dry hills were transformed to lush emerald green, and the haze in the sky dissipated to reveal blue perfection. Freedom blinked rapidly as if blinded by the sudden change, and he rubbed one wing over his eyes.

All the tension drained out of Mariel as Gabe and the Zookeeper galloped out of sight. Her mission was over. She had done all she could do. Her grip on the gate loosened, and she slid downwards, landing with a sharp cry as her wounded ankle hit the ground. Her knees gave out and she crumpled in a little heap beside the eagle.

"Easy there, milady. It's all, all right now." Freedom spread a huge wing over her to protect her from the sunlight.

Mariel's eyes remained closed. The blood on her ankle had since dried on the hem of her jeans, and the denim was stiff; but it didn't matter. Nothing mattered anymore—not even the distant three-beat gait Mariel had come to associate with the sound of an approaching horse at full gallop.

Her breathing steadied until it was very shallow, and Mariel fell unconscious.

CHAPTER
NINTEEN

When Mariel woke up, she felt as if she were lying on a cloud. She felt so peaceful that, for a moment, she left her eyes closed and soaked in the atmosphere. Warm sun was shining on her face. There was a soft breeze brushing over her, spring birdsong was all around her, and if she listened hard enough, why she seemed to hear a chorus of angels singing.

Only the angelic voices sounded vaguely familiar.

Mariel slowly opened her eyes, and a world of white swirled into focus. The music had faded like the breeze. Sun was shining through the white canvas overhead. She was lying on a soft mattress under a white coverlet. Before she could figure out exactly where she was, there was a soft chuckle by her side.

"So, Sleeping Beauty wakes up at last. I was about to embark on a quest to find you a prince."

Mariel pushed herself up on her elbow and looked over at the grinning gray horse. "Simeon?"

Chuckling, the great workhorse trotted over to her, shaking his creamy mane. He pushed his nose against her shoulder. "In the flesh."

"Simeon..." Taking his head in her arms, Mariel held him close and bit back tears. "I'm sorry," she whispered.

"What for?" wondered the horse, alternately nuzzling her shoulder and nibbling playfully at her sleeve.

"For...leaving you there," returned Mariel brokenly. "I saw them...and I thought you were..."

Simeon gave her shoulder a hard shove with his great muzzle. "You saved my life."

Mariel blinked and drew back to look at him. "I did?"

Simeon gazed steadily at her. "You saved us all."

"I didn't...do anything," she stammered, unable to wrap her mind around that impossible concept. "I'm just a helpless girl..."

"You underestimate the Zookeeper, even now." Simeon gently curled his great neck around her and settled his head over her shoulder, and Mariel slumped gratefully against his mane. "You weren't helpless. You did what the Zookeeper told you to do. You completed your mission. The Zookeeper came riding in and brought with him the sun, and the dragon was blinded by it. Mike slew him."

"What about you?" wondered the anxious girl.

"You underestimate Ralph, too," said Simeon, chuckling good-naturedly. "How's your ankle?"

Mariel had forgotten about it until then. She cautiously flexed it. "It doesn't hurt," she replied, awestruck. Then she looked up at Simeon. "Ralph?"

"Ralph." Simeon grinned.

Overwhelmed, Mariel lay down again and rested her head on the pillow. "Wow," she murmured, gazing up at the white canvas ceiling and trying to comprehend what had happened. She'd flown away from the Capital on Freedom's wings, believing the world was ending in tragedy, and instead Simeon was alive and well, telling her that she was in the middle of a happy ending.

Mariel looked baffled. It was almost unreal. "You sure I woke up in the same dimension?"

A warm, booming laugh was her only answer.

"I was sort of serious," mumbled the girl. Despite herself, she was smiling.

Simeon nuzzled her cheek affectionately, tickling her with his whiskers. Mariel giggled and squirmed, and Simeon tugged gently at her shirt collar with his teeth. "I was instructed to bring you before the Zookeeper as soon as you were ready. You can rest awhile longer, if you wish."

She sat up. "Oh, no, I think I shall see him now. To know that you are all alive, and that the Zookeeper is in charge as he should be, makes me feel…young again."

"Speak for yourself," teased the workhorse, eliciting a little laugh from Mariel. "You were already young to begin with."

Laughing made her feel better, and she slid out from beneath the coverlet, dangling her feet over the side of the bed. Then she was dismayed. "But I can't see him looking like…like this." She held out the hem of her dirty T-shirt and surveyed her torn, bloodied jeans. "I wouldn't even see my own mother looking like this. I mean, look at me. I look like...like I've been an extra in a war movie where the makeup artists went insane."

Simeon chuckled and nudged her with his soft nose. "No, actually you look worse."

Mariel gasped and shoved his head away with a mock glare. "Oh, thanks!"

Simeon grinned and nosed her again. "You're just a princess in disguise."

An incredulous grin pushed through Mariel's defenses. "You really think I look like a princess?" she wondered hopefully.

Simeon narrowed his brown eyes and studied her. "Hmm...it's a very good disguise."

Mariel pretended to sulk. "You really do know how to flatter a lady, don't you?"

The huge horse gave a mild shrug of his shoulders. "Natural charm, my dear. I was born with it."

A sudden wave of giggles arose and overtook Mariel before she could stop them. "I can't argue with you, especially since you're telling the truth. I've never met anyone who could insult me so badly and still have my complete respect and unconditional love."

The horse's twinkling brown eyes grew serious, and Mariel's laughter faded. For a long moment they gazed at each other. Neither said a word, but the words in their eyes were enough. Then Simeon spoke. "Thus are friendships forged in the heat of battle. You'll always be a princess to me, Mariel Stone, even if no one else can see it. Remember that."

Mariel's chin trembled, and she thought of the people back home. Green Valley seemed like a distant memory after her journey through the Menagerie, but now that the war was over and the Zookeeper had been restored to his rightful place, she was beginning to think of her old life—and the people who had been in it. Suddenly, their opinions didn't seem to matter so much. Her heart warmed, and silently she leaned over to hug Simeon's head.

"Thank you," she whispered.

She felt the great horse swallow hard. He didn't answer. Then he withdrew his head from her embrace and gave her a little smile and a nod that was almost shy. "But tonight, everyone will see you're a princess." He tossed his nose in the direction of one of the tent poles behind Mariel.

Turning, the girl gave a short cry of delight. A white silk dress, shot throughout with threads of gold, hung on the pole and fluttered slightly in the wind. It was the most beautiful gown Mariel had ever seen. Never mind what Simeon said about a princess; the wearer of that gown would be a *queen*. Awestruck, she rose and went to stand before it. She hesitated a moment before touching it with tentative fingers.

Then she was overwhelmed. She took a step backwards. "Oh, Simeon, I couldn't…"

The horse moved towards the open tent flap and rolled one brown eye in her direction, and Mariel fancied he looked almost sly. "Of course you can. It is a gift from a friend, though you don't have to wear it. You could always appear before the Zookeeper in the clothes you already have." Simeon laughed at Mariel's expression of dismay, and shaking his creamy mane in triumph, he trotted confidently out of the tent.

When she was alone, Mariel gazed at the dress that had been given her and hesitantly touched it with her fingertips. It seemed too grand a thing for her. Even as she thought that, she realized that everything in life had been too grand for a simple girl like her. Being chosen as a servant of the Zookeeper to carry out his most important mission and ultimately saving the

Menagerie. She couldn't comprehend that she had saved the Menagerie as Simeon had said. It was a truth and a reality she simply couldn't embrace.

The sound of light contact against the tent canvas got Mariel's attention, and she turned to see a familiar young girl in a green dress poking her head inside, pushing a waterfall of ash-blonde hair out of her eyes as she peered around. A dun-colored mule stood patiently behind her with a good-naturedly bored droop to his long ears.

"Lexi!" Mariel ran forward and embraced her. "What are you doing here?"

Lexi laughed and returned the hug, then drew back to smile up at Mariel. "Did you see the grass?" she cried exuberantly, nearly jumping up and down in her excitement. "It's green! It's all green! The Zookeeper came back and everything's great. Can you believe it?"

Mariel blinked in baffled surprise, and she looked outside the tent to survey the grass. Sure enough, it was green, but it took another moment for the full impact of Lexi's words to sink in. Everything in the Menagerie had been dull when Mariel first arrived. Now that the sun had returned, the world was full of vivid color and bursting with life as if it were the beginning of spring.

"Oh yes...yes, it's great!" put in Mariel belatedly. "It looks like it rained."

"Oh, did it ever!" Lexi twirled, and her green skirt flew around her like the ruffles on a muffin cup. "It rained and rained and rained for days, and then the sun came out again."

Mariel was shocked. "You mean... I was out for several days?"

"You were pretty tired," the girl explained with a sunny smile.

No wonder I—and the whole world—feel different, Mariel mused. Then she shook it all away and gazed at Lexi quizzically. "What are *you* doing here?"

Lexi giggled. "I was sent to help you." She motioned at the mule behind her, who was bearing a brace with two buckets of water on his back.

Mariel's gaze softened. "You were sent to help me long ago, Lexi."

Lexi panicked. "What! No I wasn't! I just heard the word that you were awake a moment ago, and I hurried over as fast as I—"

Mercifully, Mariel interrupted and took the girl by the shoulders. "I'm not talking about a hot bath, though I'd be immensely grateful for one of those about now. I meant back at the inn."

Lexi's agitation gave way to bafflement. "I…didn't draw a hot bath for you at the inn," she answered slowly, her mind racing.

Mariel smiled and shook her head at the girl's puzzled look, "You didn't know, and you may not understand even now, but the Menagerie owes this day to you." Lexi's eyes were widening in confused delight, and her expression made Mariel want to laugh. For Lexi's sake, she refrained. "By the time I reached your lovely inn, I was ready to turn back and go home, regardless of what the Zookeeper had asked of me. Something you said…changed my mind."

Lexi stood there in a shocked stupor, speechless. Suddenly, she let loose such a cacophony of ear-piercing shrieks and squeals that Mariel instantly regretted her decision to tell Lexi of her role in saving the Menagerie, as it endangered her ears. *And my immediate health,* Mariel thought ruefully as the excited girl embraced her in a wild hug of joy. But now Mariel was laughing.

Later, Mariel couldn't quite recall how she survived. But she managed to extricate herself from Lexi's clutches, and after taking her bath and changing into the beautiful white-and-gold gown, Mariel emerged from the tent with an admiring Lexi behind her, and found Simeon waiting for them.

The old horse's gaze softened when he saw her. Tucking a foreleg, he dropped into an equine bow before Mariel, thoroughly embarrassing her. But the horse was very serious. "Will you grant me the honor of bearing you once more?" he queried in a deep, husky voice.

Mariel darted forward at once and knelt down beside him, a lock of still-wet hair slapping her cheek. "Will you please stop this, Simeon? I couldn't have done anything without you, and anyway, what I did wasn't that big of a deal."

Simeon lifted his head and turned his gaze fully onto hers. "Then you don't know what you've done," he said, his tone more serious than Mariel had ever heard it. "Climb up and I'll show you."

Frowning, Mariel accepted his offer and sat down on the familiar broad back, arranging her full skirt neatly over her legs. "All right," she responded grudgingly. "As long as you know that *I'm* the one who is honored to be carried by you."

Simeon swiveled an ear in her direction, but he lurched to his hooves and trotted off without answering. Lexi, riding the good-natured mule, fell in behind them.

As Mariel looked around her, the sights were so amazing that she soon forgot to feel uncomfortable with the idea of riding on Simeon's back. Her white tent was one of dozens that had been pitched on a flat clearing. All of them were white to keep the occupants from overheating. The wind caught in the open door-flaps, and snapped away as delightfully as the multicolored pennants and banners set up on poles beside each tent. Grass glittered as brightly as emeralds with tiny diamond-like raindrops still glistening on them after the recent storm had swept through. Dandelions, daisies and violets were scattered at Simeon's hooves, and the trees surrounding the clearing swayed in a gentle rhythm to the soft breeze. The sky overhead was so brilliant and blue that Mariel could scarcely look at it without hurting her eyes.

The impromptu camp was silent as the little company moved through it, along a lane of trampled grass between the rows of white tents, but Mariel didn't feel as one traveling through a ghost town might. There was no sense of loss or loneliness, but only peace and an undercurrent of joy. It took her a moment to realize that this atmosphere was greatly contributed to by the birdsong rising around them.

"I hear music," Mariel remarked. Behind her, Lexi giggled, and Mariel shot the other girl a quizzical glance. "I thought I heard angels singing, too."

"You'll see presently," Simeon put in before Lexi could say anything. Lexi was still giggling, much to Mariel's puzzlement.

When they reached the edge of the clearing and looked down over the valley, Mariel caught her breath. The place was alive with celebrating creatures dancing all down the hill, many of them playing musical instruments and creating a symphony of what seemed to be well-known anthems, because every last animal knew the melodies and the words.

Creatures were arriving in streams from every direction, and before Mariel knew it they were caught in the midst of the joyful parade. Flocks of birds with brilliant plumage flew over the processions, twittering in their little bird-voices and singing in a language even Mariel could understand.

Lost in wonder, Mariel's wide eyes traveled over the sea of animals all migrating towards the Capital. Herds of camels flowed in from the west, and Mariel marveled. She'd never seen a camel before outside of a television program or a textbook.

Then another kind of creature's thin head poked over the hill, and Mariel all but forgot the camels. The strange head was followed by a long, cream-and-burgundy splotched neck, and it grew taller over the whole gathering of animals until it materialized as a giraffe. Other members of the same species followed close behind it.

There were animals Mariel couldn't begin to put names to in that parade.

"Mongooses," Simeon supplied as a whole flock of ferret-like creatures rushed down the hillside, somehow avoiding the hooves of animals that would have otherwise trampled them. "Tapirs," he added, nodding at what looked like large pigs with sawed-off elephant's trunks. "And capybaras." Beaver-like rodents with perpetual smiles went running past, drawing a squeal of delight from Lexi. She bounced on the back of her placid mule.

Mariel thought her head would spin. She couldn't keep the various species and their names straight. Just then, she heard her own name being shouted over the music and laughter and the cacophony of animal noises.

"Mariel! Mariel!"

The girl twisted on Simeon's back, peering through the crowd to see who was calling her name. When several tiny voices joined the chant, she lowered her vision to the ground and found six spiny hedgehogs running after Simeon as fast as their short legs could carry them.

Mariel drew a gasp of excitement. "Ben! Marcy! Oh, Simeon, stop!" The startled horse flung up his head as his passenger slid swiftly to the ground, smoothing her skirt and hurrying towards the little hedgehog family.

Ben reached her first and hopped up, putting his front paws against her shins and smiling up at her. "You made it! Congratulations."

"Thanks in part to you," Mariel responded, crouching down to their level with a bright smile. "And thanks to this." From behind her ear, she drew the little forget-me-not, which remarkably hadn't wilted yet. She twirled it between her fingers, and Joey came trundling up to her and took a giant whiff of the blue flower. Then he sneezed.

"Oh, dear, Joey. Still suffering from that cold?" wondered Mariel.

Puffing slightly, Marcy came up after her hedgehog son and gave a sheepish chuckle. "He has allergies, too," she explained.

Mariel giggled, then turned as she felt a little tug on the side of her skirt. Jordyce was there, blushing bright red through her cream-colored fur.

"I... I... I made you this," Jordyce said shyly, holding up one end of a long daisy chain which trailed three feet behind her.

The perky white flowers were a little worn from being dragged over the ground all day, but Mariel reacted as if Jordyce had given her a strand of pearls and garnets. "This is gorgeous!" she exalted, winding the daisies around her neck and tying off the ends. "And it matches my dress. See?"

Jordyce flushed with pleasure and hid behind her mother.

Gary toddled up to her next, his cheeks puffed out like a squirrel's, and he sat down and grinned up at Mariel while he chewed. He plucked the leaves from a nearby dandelion. "Ishn't 'is great?" he queried in between mouthfuls. "Flowers is growin' everywhere!"

For the first time, Mariel looked about her at the wildflowers with true appreciation. They were growing above ground everywhere now that the Zookeeper had returned. The significance had been lost on her before. She took wildflowers for granted in the world she came from.

Understanding dawned in her eyes, and she exchanged a joyful glance with Ben before answering Gary. "You're going to turn into a little butterball if you keep stuffing yourself full of leaves!"

Gary grinned and snatched another leaf, obviously not caring one whit. Already, he'd put on some weight, Mariel was glad to see. Joey and Davy sat beside their brother and grinned.

"We've moved out of our old hole to a place just outside the City of Gold," Ben told her. "I'm getting a new job digging truffles and ginger-roots. It pays much better than flower-digging."

"That's great news," gushed Mariel, standing up suddenly and gazing over the throngs of animals. No wonder the air rang with song! She wondered how many of them had similar stories to tell, all related to the return of the Zookeeper.

Then she couldn't wait to see the Zookeeper for herself. Whirling, the girl ran back to Simeon, who obligingly laid down in the grass until Mariel clambered aboard. The procession started again, and Mariel fed him one of the daisies that fell from Jordyce's necklace. She giggled when his whiskers tickled her hand.

"You can't help growing whiskers when you get old like me," said the horse with a grin.

Mariel laughed. "I can't quite imagine myself with whiskers."

"I can't either, Mariel."

Beside them, a kangaroo pricked her ears, and she stared at the girl on Simeon's back. "Oh, my…" She gasped and nudged her companion. "That's her! That's Mariel Stone!"

There was a short pause. "Did you say Mariel Stone?"

A buzz of Mariel's name rippled through the crowd like wildfire as Mariel watched with widening eyes. Animal heads swiveled in their direction and eyes of all shapes and sizes followed Simeon's placid progress. The music faltered and faded away, and a hushed awe fell over the gathering. The forward march ceased and, in the ensuing traffic jam, Simeon was forced to stop.

Dead silence fell over the valley. Mariel swallowed hard, feeling a thousand stares riveted on her—all stares from the animal kingdom, which was even more unnerving than the stares of a human audience. Some of those animals were deadly predators in their natural habitat, and they were all watching her.

They seemed to be waiting. Mariel felt as if she had to say something.

"Um…hi," she attempted, giving a halfhearted wave.

A soft murmur of admiration ran through the crowd as if she had just delivered a speech of great historical note. Rolling his eyes, Simeon craned his head around and bumped his nose against her knee.

"Er…long live the Zookeeper!" Mariel burst out.

This was greeted by a magnanimous cheer—or what was really a wild confusion of stamping and braying and roaring and screeching—and a thrill rose in Mariel's chest. Lifting her hand and her flared sleeve like a banner, she cried, "To the Capital! To the Zookeeper!"

The animals surged forward eagerly as the music began again—a perky, joyous tune that accompanied the procession out of the valley, over the flatland that had been the site of a battlefield and was now fresh and green and growing with wild-flowers, and through the city gates on a pathway littered with flower petals. From the highest towers of the Capital, confetti fluttered down from the hands of the stone angels onto the hundreds of animals pouring through the streets. Mariel was laughing, and she held out her hands to catch the paper rain, letting it land on her arms and drift through her fingers.

She felt as if she were living in a dream.

Mike and his flaming stallion fell into place ahead of them, and the great warrior held aloft a great gold banner with the symbol of a fiery dove upon it. He glanced back and caught Mariel's eyes, and his bold expression softened into a smile.

The lane became too crowded to continue further on horseback, so Mike dismounted and helped Mariel to the ground. Then, with Simeon right behind her, they went along single-file through the crush until they reached a clearing. Mariel realized it was the place where the building holding the key and the scroll once stood, but there was no sign of it. Every last stone was gone as if the building had never been there.

She turned aside to ask Simeon about it, and let out a muffled shriek instead. "Anna!" She ran forward to hug the llama, burrowing her face against Anna's fluffy fur.

Anna turned her head and gently nuzzled the girl's ear. "Hello, little one," she greeted softly.

After a moment, Mariel stepped back to look at Anna. The cream-colored llama was cream-colored again; all the mud and dust had been washed out of her beautiful fur, and she looked like the llama Mariel had met when she first entered the Menagerie. Gone was the tired look from her eyes, which were warm and sparkling as they returned Mariel's curious gaze.

"You look...great!" Mariel burst out. "Where have you been? What happened?"

"Watching over you and Simeon, for a long time," returned Anna with calm satisfaction in her voice. "I assisted Ralph and cared for many of the injured. Then the Zookeeper had need of me."

"Wow, what for?"

Anna chuckled. "Coordinating—"

"A feast!" screeched the seagull Marcus, who came hurtling out of the sky at that moment and landed hard on Anna's fluffy back. Anna, to her credit, merely flicked an ear at him. "And I'm *starving*! Do you know how far I've had to fly these last few days?"

"All the way to the Other Side, no doubt," broke in the black panther Adelle, padding up to them with her unnerving emerald eyes fixed on the bird, "while the rest of us went to war. You had the easy job."

"Easy, my beak!" Marcus ruffled his feathers, indignant. "Easy for you to say! *You* didn't have to fly across the whole Menagerie just to give the Zookeeper his cue for the grand entrance! You were marching around, singing the walls down!"

"Singing?" put in Gabe, striding up to the little congregating group. Mariel brightened when she saw him, and Gabe returned her smile, then focused his attention on the discomfited seagull. "If you think singing is *easy...*" He nodded conspiratorially in the direction of Ralph, who was standing off to one side, frowning into the large mug of steaming liquid he was holding. "He's avoiding speaking to anyone just now," Gabe explained in a lowered voice.

"Why?" queried Mariel, thinking Ralph was not the least bit antisocial.

"Because he lost his voice."

Mariel choked on her laughter even as she shot a sympathetic glance at the healer whom she was indebted to for the second time. "Poor fellow!"

"Voices come back in a day or two," scoffed Marcus, waving a wing dismissively at Ralph. "All he needs is a wee bit of rest."

Mariel was laughing. "Don't worry, Marcus, you also can have all the rest you need now that the Zookeeper is back."

Marcus sent her a disgusted look. "Rest? Ha! I don't need rest. You know what I need?" He flared his scraggly wings. "New *feathers*!"

The small company erupted in laughter. Mariel took the opportunity to glance around at the diverse gathering of friends—a panther, a family of hedgehogs, a workhorse, a llama, a seagull, and people like Gabe, Ralph, Mike and Lexi. It was like a menagerie—her own Menagerie.

She noticed Lexi's father, Chuck, standing beside a woman Mariel correctly guessed was Lexi's mother Leann, and her bright smile and her wave were returned—and then she was interrupted when Gabe caught her hand and brought her attention back to the group.

"Well, then, let's just ask the Zookeeper for those new feathers." While everyone else was paralyzed, wondering whether Gabe was joking, Gabe swept Mariel a deep bow and tucked her hand through the crook of his elbow. "Will you do the honor of allowing me to escort you to the Zookeeper's table?"

Mariel blushed, lowering her eyes, but she was smiling. "Certainly."

"Thank you, milady." He drew her gently to his side, then turned his smiling gaze back to the company. "And now, if you will follow us…"

He strode forward with great dignity while Mariel's friends fell in behind them. Marcus was still complaining. "Ask the Zookeeper for new feathers? He's addled! Does he have any idea how long it takes to *grow* new feathers? No, of course not," he answered his own rhetorical question. "He's never had wings!"

Gabe suddenly burst out laughing. Mariel looked at up him quizzically, wondering what he found so amusing. But Gabe only gave her one of his winning smiles as he led her through the crowd, which was clustered here and there in small groups. Animals and people alike were all chattering happily.

Suddenly, Mariel caught her breath and came to a stop, her jaw agape at the incredible sight before her.

CHAPTER TWENTY

There were three enormous tables covered in glimmering gold tablecloths, and silver-covered dishes were set from end to end on each one. Each place setting featured a gold swan-folded napkin resting on a gold plate beside a jewel-encrusted golden goblet, and the silverware was made of real silver. Already seated at the table were an incredible variety of animals, ranging from squirrels and chipmunks to Hunter, the grizzly bear, who didn't need a chair. Neither did Freedom the eagle, who stood next to him ignoring the stares of the same squirrels and chipmunks. And no wonder. He was nearly the size of the grizzly.

Mariel hardly noticed. It was the Zookeeper himself who took her breath away.

It was hard to believe that he'd once been the old, bent man tending the lovely garden outside the black gate, because now he looked like a young man, and Mariel wondered whether it was merely an illusion. Seated beside Mike, he was arrayed in a white suit trimmed with braided gold. Mike must have just told him a joke, because the Zookeeper suddenly burst into spontaneous, rippling laughter that warmed Mariel all over.

That's when he saw her. He glanced in her direction, then did a double-take and arose from his chair, gazing at her with a soft smile. Wordlessly, Mariel dropped into a graceful curtsy beside the bowing Gabe, and with a gesture of his lordly hand the Zookeeper bade them to rise. "Be seated," he invited, indicating the chair immediately to his right. Gabe escorted her to the high table and pulled out her chair, and Mariel sat down beside the Zookeeper himself.

It was all she could do to keep from staring. The Zookeeper looked so *different*, so young and vibrant, that she wouldn't have known him were it not for his familiar brown eyes, which now radiated joy. Mariel was so nervous already that she could hardly stand to look at him, so she studied her gold folded napkin swan resting on her gold plate instead. It was made of real silk, just like the tablecloth.

The Zookeeper noticed and, with a slight smile, he leaned over to her. "Don't worry. You don't have to eat him," he assured her.

"I know," put in Mariel quickly, her eyes darting to his. "I was just…"

Abruptly, she caught the humor in his gaze, and she giggled. The Zookeeper's warm laugh joined hers, and the tension Mariel felt in the company of such greatness dissipated—as the Zookeeper no doubt intended.

Then he stood up, and at once a hush descended over the gathering. He picked up a curious gold circlet from beside his empty plate. A large sapphire was set in the center of it, and before Mariel could wonder what it was the Zookeeper reached over and settled it onto her head. The sapphire gleamed on her forehead.

"I give you our queen!" pronounced the Zookeeper, and Mariel's stomach leaped into her throat. The crowd burst into applause, and Mariel's eyes darted up to the Zookeeper, full of questions.

"Does this mean that I…that I can't go home?" she queried, her voice soft and shaky.

"It means that this is your home," answered the Zookeeper, gazing at her with incredible warmth in his eyes. "And you will see it again, someday. In the meantime, you can go back to where you live."

Mariel thought of her distant Green Valley memories, and of her parents—who should be returning from vacation in the morning, she realized. "I think I would like to go back," she said carefully. "But I…thank you…and yet I don't have the first clue of how to be a good queen." The title of queen felt strange to her as it left her lips.

The Zookeeper smiled. "All in good time, my dear. Trust me."

Once Mariel relaxed again, the Zookeeper turned his attention to his guests—primarily Marcus. The blustery young seagull had fallen silent when actually confronted with the Zookeeper himself, but fortunately he was perched on Anna's withers and the llama carried him to the Zookeeper's table. It took some coaxing, but the Zookeeper managed to get Marcus to make the short hop from Anna's back to the fine gold table-cloth. Marcus stood there, his head nervously jerking from side to side while his neck shrunk turtle-like into the rest of his body, and his wings gave an occasional twitch. Mariel actually felt sorry for him.

The Zookeeper reached for him, and Marcus cringed and closed his eyes, bracing himself. But the Zookeeper's hands were gentle. He carefully smoothed the feathers on Marcus' wings.

"What's the trouble, little Marcus?" the Zookeeper queried, still brushing his fingers lightly over Marcus' wings.

The seagull opened his eyes and relaxed, much like Mariel had done. He looked up at the Zookeeper as all his fear melted away, and a shy little smile tugged at the corners of his beak.

"Oh, I…it's not too bad, really." The Zookeeper released him, and Marcus spread his raggedy wings to show the Zookeeper the gaps between the sparse feathers. "I've been doing a lot of flying lately and I lost some of my—"

He broke off with a gasp, and Mariel stared. Now, Marcus wasn't missing a single feather that Mariel could tell, and his perfect wings shone brightly as if brand-new. The Zookeeper was laughing in his heartwarming way. "You lost your power of speech, is what you lost, my little friend. Perhaps some food will restore your tongue? Here, come sit at my table, next to Mike. You get first dibs on the shrimp."

With that, streams of smiling servants bearing dishes poured out from one of the stone buildings, and after the Zookeeper prayed a brief and very joyful grace, the feasting began with hungry enthusiasm. Exuberant chatter filled the air. A tall white crane struck up a full orchestra of animals playing instruments. The crane conducted the symphony with sweeping movements of his graceful wings, and Mariel wondered if even music in heaven could compare. Men dressed in gold-silk uniforms took their places before the Zookeeper's table, and Mariel started in fright, turning a shade paler. They were the soldiers from the City of Gold.

Gabe noticed her unease and leaned over to her. "Don't worry. They've been set free and serve the Zookeeper now."

Mariel watched them warily despite Gabe's assurances. "Are you saying they were slaves before?"

"In a manner of speaking, yes."

The former soldiers certainly seemed happier, and they indeed put on a lovely show for the Zookeeper, performing acrobatics and forming human pyramids and juggling flaming torches. Mariel was so dazzled that for a while she forgot to eat, and when the first act was over, she clapped and cheered enthusiastically. To her surprise, the entire company of men lined up before the Zookeeper's table and bowed first to the Zookeeper, and then to her in a gesture of apology. Mariel swallowed hard and nodded her head in return as a gesture of forgiveness.

Then her stomach loudly reminded her that she was starving.

As each course was served on silver platters and passed down the tables, Mariel smiled at the memory of the food she'd longed for when she first entered the Menagerie. The Zookeeper's feast made her wildest dreams seem a beggar's ration by comparison. She started with the most incredible fettuccini Alfredo and tasted lobster for the first time. Then she tried the shrimp—what little of it was left after it passed Marcus' plate—and found it delicious. She sampled the salmon and the swordfish, finding both unique and delicious, but opting for Leann's famous cheese and spinach casserole instead. Spinach hadn't formerly been one of Mariel's favorite foods, but since she'd eaten it at the Sign of the Times when she was reunited with Simeon and Anna, she'd changed her mind about it.

Once she'd had her fill of the main courses and moved on to dessert, which included everything from blackberry cream tarts and cinnamon raisin bread to plum pudding, Mariel was beyond stuffed.

"I feel as if I'll never have to eat again," she said in an aside to Gabe.

Gabe chuckled. "I'll help by taking this cherry crepe off your hands," he replied, smiling innocently as he stole the crepe.

Mariel shot him an indignant glare, but she was powerless against his charming smile and she knew it. "You're welcome," she retorted dryly. "And how about a lemon square?"

"Don't mind if I do," Gabe responded smoothly, relocating the lemon square to his own plate. Then he soothed Mariel's feelings by offering her a chocolate strawberry and a little dish of chilled crème brûlée.

Mariel warmed all over. "Thanks for reminding me why I should be glad I never had a brother," she told him with a smile.

Gabe caught her gaze and held it. "As servants of the Zookeeper, we're all brothers and sisters." He waved his hand over the gathering. "We are a family."

Mariel suddenly couldn't breathe. She looked over the throngs of animals and men, feeling something unfamiliar yet comforting encircling her soul. As an only child, she'd never had siblings, and now she had too many of them to count.

Gabe smiled at her wondrous expression and patted her hand.

Day passed into evening before Mariel knew it, and the stars came out to shine on them. Torches were mounted on tall poles at intervals along the streets of the Capital City until it was bright as day. There was still plenty of celebration left in the party, and animals were dancing in the streets. Between the colossal stone buildings were bonfires around which eager creatures clustered to share stories and laugh and sing snatches of songs. Gabe took Mariel by the arm and helped her navigate the streets, and they roved from one bonfire to another, mingling with the celebrants.

Mariel was privileged to meet Rick again. "The birds have almost forgotten how to say gravitas, I think," he said in answer to Mariel's anxious questions. "They haven't heard it in a while, so they've picked up something else entirely, and they seem rather preoccupied with it. We have these three frogs down at the pond who, instead of croaking like normal frogs, insist on blurting out, 'Zoo-keep-errrr', over and over and over again. The birds are taking up the chorus." Rick laughed. "I'm sure it'll get old with time, but for now it's amusing. Hopefully, we'll find something else for them to screech about before we all lose our minds."

Mariel also had the chance to meet Rick's wife, Kim. "Oh, it turned out lovely!" she exclaimed, gazing rapturously at Mariel's gown. Kim and Lexi's mother, Leann, had made the gown especially for Mariel to wear at the celebration.

"We wanted it to match the Zookeeper's white-and-gold outfit," Leann explained.

At their insistence, Mariel lightly picked up her shimmering skirt and performed a graceful pirouette to show off their handiwork, drawing a chorus of oohs and ahhs from the onlookers.

"Fit for the queen of the Menagerie," Kim observed, smiling kindly.

Mariel blushed, and thanked them profusely for the dress, and she made a point to thank Leann also for her casseroles. "I'll look forward to your cooking when next I stop by the Sign of the Times."

"Our doors are always open to you," put in Chuck, who stood beside his wife with his hand resting on little Lexi's shoulder.

Gabe escorted Mariel down the torchlit path, pausing at each bonfire to allow Mariel to visit with those she'd come to know on her journey through the Menagerie—as well as complete strangers. Marcus was regaling a whole group of the younger creatures with exaggerated tales of his harrowing adventures as he carried out his dangerous missions for the Zookeeper, flaring his wings at every dramatic point in the story. Every pair of wide eyes was fixed on him, hanging on his every word.

"He talks with his wings," observed Mariel, laughing softly. "That's an Italian bird if I ever saw one."

They visited briefly with Hunter, the grizzly bear, Adelle, the black panther, and Mike, trading war stories like old veterans and laughing at themselves for it. Mariel hugged the still-silent Ralph and told him how grateful she was for all he had done for her, and poor Ralph smiled and whispered something Mariel pretended to understand. Then she questioned Freedom about his unusual height.

"Well…" Freedom fluffed his feathers importantly. "Most birds are on a strictly protein-rich diet. I ate my greens."

Mariel burst out laughing. Freedom raised one feathery eyebrow, and Mariel's laughter faltered. Suddenly, she couldn't tell whether he was joking or not, and she didn't have much incentive to press a giant fearsome-looking eagle about his eating habits.

Mariel bid Ben's family an early good night, since they had to put their children to bed, and Ben and Marcy trundled off with a line of yawning baby hedgehogs trailing behind them. Marcus flew with them. He was tired, but mostly eager to try out his new wings. Jordyce brought up the rear, and she turned to Mariel with a sleepy smile and waved her paw.

"Bye!" she called as they disappeared in the darkness.

Mariel also had a chance to get reacquainted with many of the animals she'd broken her fast with at the barn in the country, who were thanking Elaine and her daughters, Andrea and Ella, for protecting their little haven until the poor leopards were flushing rosy right through their fur.

"They were just wolves," said Elaine, regally sitting down and curling her tail around her paws with all the inherent feline grace she possessed. "Everyone knows cats are superior." But there was a sly glint in her yellow eyes which hinted to Mariel that Elaine wasn't quite serious.

"We really weren't all that brave," agreed Andrea, twitching the tip of her tail.

Ella looked as if she were hiding a grin. She winked a yellow eye at her sister. "That's right. All we *really* wanted was to protect our breakfast."

Laughter broke the tension in the circle, and the modest leopards seemed enormously grateful for a change of subject.

Lastly, Gabe and Mariel strolled up to Simeon the Noble and Anna the Wise, who were waiting alone by the bonfire nearest the city gates. A lump rose in Mariel's throat when she caught the sorrowful look in their soft brown eyes, and suddenly it hit her. She was leaving them. Trembling, she unconsciously gripped Gabe's arm, and Gabe put his arm comfortingly around her shoulders.

Swallowing hard, Mariel moved away from Gabe and stood before the llama, looking her directly in the eyes. The silence that passed between them was filled with memories of the past few days. Then Mariel stepped forward and hugged Anna, burying her face in the soft fur.

"Anna," she whispered thickly, "I'm going to miss you."

"Not as much as I'll miss you, little one," said the llama, nuzzling Mariel's shoulder.

For a while, they stood together, Mariel crying as Anna whispered secrets in the girl's ear, Mariel nodding her understanding into the cream-colored neck.

At last Mariel drew away, wiping her cheeks as she gave Anna a tearful smile. "I'll never forget you, I promise."

"Nor will I, little one."

Mariel turned to Simeon next, and after another moment of memory-filled silence, she hugged him and wept again while the old workhorse rubbed his velveteen nose against her back.

"You be a good girl," he murmured at length. He didn't sound quite himself.

"I will," Mariel promised, stepping back and brushing away fresh tears. Then she looked up at him. "Will I see you again?"

Simeon lifted his head higher. "Count on it, little feather," he replied, using the nickname he'd given her at the start of their journey. "In the meantime, you will always have me in your heart...as you will be in mine."

Mariel smiled sadly, but the words made her feel less sad. Gabe took her arm and led her slowly away, and Mariel didn't look back.

They stepped beyond the gates, and North Star was waiting for them, gleaming faintly against a backdrop of black sky and diamond stars. The Zookeeper himself was standing beside the white stallion, resplendent in his white-and-gold uniform.

"Mariel Stone," He said softly, taking both her hands in his as she came to him. He gazed deep into her eyes. "Thank you," He said sincerely.

Mariel smiled back at him. "It is you who gave me the gift," she answered. "Now I understand why you sent me on this journey and why it had to be so difficult. Thank you, so much, for choosing me."

The Zookeeper beamed. When Mariel looked at North Star, she found Gabe already astride. He held down a hand for her, then whisked her onto the stallion's back, folding his arms around her. Mariel settled herself, then glanced back at the Zookeeper. He was standing before the gate of the city she'd helped restore to him, and Mariel thought he looked as if he'd been standing there for thousands of years—as if he belonged there.

And then North Star leapt away, and they were flying with the wind, racing into a starry night. Mariel watched the Zookeeper grow smaller and smaller until he disappeared altogether, and North Star rounded a bend, robbing her of the sight of the Capital city, gleaming with all its brilliant torches.

A full stomach combined with emotional exhaustion and relief worked like a soothing tonic on Mariel's body, and before she knew it her head was nodding. Gabe held her close as she drifted off to sleep.

CHAPTER
TWENTY-ONE

Mariel's eyes blinked open, and she saw, as if through a dull haze, what looked like her own familiar bedroom. She was no longer on the horse, but cradled in the comforting gentleness of Gabe's arms, and he laid her down carefully on her own bed. With a tired mumble, Mariel snuggled her cheek into the cool pillow.

Gabe pressed a kiss to her forehead. "Goodbye, Chosen One," he murmured softly.

Sudden aching clenched Mariel's heart. He was leaving her. She reached out a weary hand and clasped his, struggling for coherence, but her subconscious was fighting her. She could feel it. Lacy gray fuzz edged her vision, giving everything a glowing dreamlike quality. Gabe looked like an angel.

"Gabe," she whimpered, "please don't leave me."

For a moment he stood over her, her small hand weakly resting in his palm, and he gazed at her with sympathy in his blue eyes. "You'll be fine, little one. You're home. This is where you belong."

"Gabe..." Mariel struggled against her heavy eyelids, which pressed down on her like twin anvils, and she saw Gabe's jaw tighten. He pressed her hand between both of his, then set it on the quilt as if it were made of something very fragile. Mariel choked on a sob. "Gabe, no," she whispered.

"I have to go," Gabe told her softly, his voice heavy with regret. He tried to smile. "Everything's going to be all right..."

"Gabe..." Terror rose dimly in some part of her mind, but it wasn't enough to wake her or to loosen the oppressive grasp of sleep over her. Sleep seemed like a living presence, and it had her firmly in its grip like a dragon with a helpless victim, paralyzing her limbs. Mariel couldn't summon the strength to wriggle free as it pulled her inexorably toward the black void of unconsciousness. Her cries were becoming more feeble as her vision of Gabe dimmed. "No, please, stay...stay..."

Gabe backed a step toward the doorway, but he got no farther than that. His jaw tightened again, and Mariel knew he didn't want to go, either. *Then why don't you stay? Why don't you help me?* her helpless mind pleaded.

For a moment, Gabe looked down at the carpet, and then his eyes met hers. "I'm sorry, Mariel, but I will come for you again someday," he added quickly—a promise to both himself and to her, for both their sakes.

A tear slid down Mariel's unresisting cheek as a terrible sense of loss spiraled through her, but she could do nothing about it. Sleep rose up ruthlessly and claimed her against her will. She managed to form a single word, to call his name one more time. "Gabe," she whispered brokenly as darkness claimed her vision altogether, stealing her last glimpse of the Zookeeper's faithful servant. As if from far away, she saw him lift his hand and slowly wave goodbye.

Mariel descended into sleep. She could feel herself falling. She couldn't fight it. It was as if her will had been taken from her and she was simply floating at the whim of some greater force beyond her control. But she was devastated. Even as she hovered in the weightlessness of space somewhere between where she was and where she was going, Mariel's throat ached with the need to sob. Her heart was torn with pain. Darkness slowly clouded her thoughts as well, sending her ever deeper into sleep.

"Gabe," she whispered as it consumed her altogether, "please don't go…"

CHAPTER
TWENTY-TWO

The melodic chatter of birdsong brought Mariel out of her deep sleep. Pale morning sunlight poured through the window and the air smelled of fresh rain.

Mariel lay beneath the warmth of her quilt, letting her conflicting emotions settle in. She was home again, and she already missed her new friends—no, her new family, she corrected herself. A lingering sense of triumph remained after the difficult journey she'd undertaken to restore the Zookeeper as king of the Menagerie. Just as she was wondering how she was going to explain a missing pair of jeans to her parents, since her outfit had been ruined beyond repair by the battle, she idly trailed a hand to her sleeve to caress the fine material of her lovely gown…and found that it was gone.

Mariel sat bolt upright, suddenly awake. She was wearing sweats and a T-shirt.

It was just a dream?

Her heart beginning to pound, she cast a glance out the window. In the soft light of dawn, the world looked freshly washed from the storm. Mariel's head whipped around, and she found her bedside lamp exactly where it should have been. The clothes she had worn to school were still heaped in an unceremonious pile.

"There is *no* way I could have dreamed all that!" she cried aloud, almost panicked. She could see them all so clearly: Gabe, sitting in her kitchen and nursing a lump on his head after breaking into her house; Anna, chasing her around the placid Simeon while they were on the road to the Avian Jungle; battling off an entire pack of evil wolves in the Chamber of the Nine Judges; flying on a huge eagle's back to the black gate to let in the Zookeeper and riding through the night on North Star's back as he carried her back home.

"It *did* happen. It wasn't a dream!" she repeated emphatically, as if stating it would make it true. But the awful feeling that it *was* only a dream was creeping over her, and Mariel bit her lip as a deep sense of loss settled in. They were her friends, her new family…

Distraught, she rubbed a hand over her forehead—and stopped. Her fingers closed over something thin and coldly metallic. Reaching up slowly, almost reverently, Mariel lifted the thin gold circlet from her head and stared at the sapphire until it blurred with tears of joy and relief.

She wasn't quite sure how a dreamworld—or what appeared to be a dreamworld—could be real, but she didn't question it. She was too delighted to contemplate the logic of it. What a mercy that she still had her crown!

She drew a shattered breath and hugged the crown close for a moment. "Thank God," she whispered. Then she swung her legs out from beneath the sheets and padded across the carpet in her bare feet, and hid the little crown in the top drawer of her dresser. Somehow, this secret was too precious to share.

So there really was a Menagerie and a Zookeeper, and she'd been through a war. Mariel chuckled ruefully to herself and swept a hand through her dark hair. This sure wasn't something many girls her age had experienced.

Feeling a sudden need to preserve the memories while they were still fresh in her mind, Mariel fished a sketchpad out of her closet and plucked a pair of pencils from her bedstand before leaving her room. She'd barely seated herself at the kitchen table and begun the rudimentary outline of a great horse's head when she heard a knock at the door.

Mariel leapt from her chair. "They're home!" she cried, and she ran to the front door and threw it open. It wasn't Mariel's parents, as she'd thought. Standing on the front porch, shifting her feet somewhat nervously and tucking her hands in the pockets of her jeans, was Beth.

"Oh…hi," began Mariel awkwardly. She cleared her throat. "Would…would you like to come in?"

"Um…if you don't mind too much," mumbled Beth, risking a glance at Mariel. Mariel gave her a little smile, and Beth was encouraged enough to step inside the doorway. "Er…thanks."

"Would you like some coffee?" Mariel questioned amiably, already starting for the kitchen.

Beth closed the front door and shuffled after her, twirling a lock of blonde hair. There were deep purple circles beneath her eyes, Mariel realized with a start. "Sure, if you don't mind too much," she answered quietly.

"I'm going to have some," returned Mariel with forced cheerfulness. "It's no trouble."

Beth slid into a chair at the table and swallowed. "Oh, thank you." There was an uncomfortable silence while Mariel set the coffee brewing. With some reluctance, she rejoined Beth and sat down opposite her. Beth was studying the sketch.

"Nice picture," she commented.

"I just started on it."

"He looks pretty good, already."

"But he hasn't even got eyes yet."

Beth went back to twirling her hair. "I know, but still. He just…looks good."

Mariel picked up a pencil and began spinning it through her fingers, her eyes on the drawing and her thoughts on the real Simeon. "Thanks."

The continuous drip from the sputtering coffeemaker seemed quite loud as both girls were at a loss for conversational topics. In desperation, Beth looked out the window.

"Quite a storm last night," she remarked in a tone intended to be casual.

Mariel had had enough. "You didn't come here to discuss the weather, Beth."

Beth turned wide green eyes to her best friend. "How did you know?"

Mariel shrugged and looked away, hiding a smile. Beth was actually serious.

Beth rubbed the back of her neck. "Well…okay. I didn't sleep last night."

"I gathered," put in Mariel with a wry smile. When Beth glanced up at her questioningly, Mariel added, "You look absolutely terrible."

Beth looked shocked. "I do?"

Mariel nodded emphatically. "Like an ogre," she said. "I barely recognized you on my front porch!"

Beth looked so horrified that Mariel giggled. Beth suddenly realized that her friend was teasing her, and they laughed together like a couple of grade-schoolers. The choking tension in the air evaporated.

"Ah, thank you," Beth finally remarked, getting her mirth under control. Abruptly, she grew deadly serious. "Mars, there's something I have to tell you."

Mariel sobered as well and leaned back in her chair, watching Beth intently.

"I did some checking on the Internet last night," Beth began, her words flowing more freely. "Turns out you had all your facts straight."

"Oh…which facts?" To Mariel, yesterday seemed a lifetime ago.

"The…you know, about protection. It's not really much protection against…against anything."

Mariel rose and crossed the kitchen, fetching a pair of mugs from the cupboard. "What exactly did you find out?"

"That condoms fail more often than not," Beth confessed. "And it doesn't prevent diseases at all. They say the pill causes cancer and that sleeping around has…emotional consequences. The evidence was pretty convincing."

"Hmm." Mariel shut off the coffeemaker and poured the dark liquid into the mugs. "Funny you should bring all this up.

I was thinking about yesterday, too, and I was considering giving Josh Greeley a call."

Beth's emerald eyes went huge. "Mars, don't you dare! After what I found out last night, how could you even *think* about it?"

"Oh…" Mariel turned her back while she found the sugar and creamer. "I was just feeling sort of…desperate, and Josh Greeley *is* a hot guy—"

"Mariel Stone!" Beth's voice had risen to a screech, and Mariel glanced over her shoulder to find the blonde out of her chair, pale-faced and upset. "Look, I was wrong, okay? Just because I said… I mean… Mars, it's a really big world, and there's lots more to life than Green Valley, and there are loads and loads of hot guys to choose from, and…what are you smiling about?" she finished indignantly, blinking angrily.

"Oh, nothing. Milk and sugar?"

Beth stomped her booted foot. "Mars, this is *not* funny!" she cried, glaring at her friend, who was leaning calmly against the counter and watching with a placid smirk as Beth's outrage escalated to unparalleled heights. "Have you been listening to me at all? How could you ignore all the *facts* and…?"

Her voice trailed off. Mariel Stone was known for being highly intelligent and unusually logical, which were both qualities that won her the best grades in Green Valley and propelled her to valedictorian status. Beth's eyes narrowed. "You're not serious."

Mariel laughed purposefully, then broke off abruptly and said, straight-faced, "No."

Beth sank into her chair and put her head in her hands as Mariel finished preparing the coffee. She returned to the table and sat one mug before the overwrought girl. "I sure had you, though," Mariel observed, grinning.

Beth shot her what was supposed to be a furious glare, but melted into a tired smile. "You're cruel, Mars."

"Alas, I know," Mariel sighed, taking a seat across from Beth and sipping cautiously at her steaming coffee. "I was born that way."

They sat awhile in companionable silence, each lost in her own thoughts. Beth studied her mug without much interest. She looked exhausted, and Mariel felt sorry for her. The poor girl had been through a lot in the last twenty-four hours.

Reaching across the table, Mariel patted Beth's hand. "I'm glad," she said softly.

"That you're cruel?" Beth glanced up with a twinkle in her eyes.

Mariel giggled. "Yes, I am. But I'm also glad that you know what I know, and that you're on my side."

Beth's expression filled with trepidation. "The rest of Green Valley won't be so easy to convince, Mars. I stayed up all night, checking and rechecking and cross-referencing all my findings. I couldn't believe what I was reading."

Mariel nodded thoughtfully. "You know this isn't a very popular viewpoint, right? You could lose all your friends over this."

The blonde scowled. "I don't care. I'm not going to screw up my life like everyone else," she added with unusual vehemence. Mariel smiled, and Beth looked up at her. "Besides, I've got you."

Mariel squeezed her hand. "Yes, you do. Best friends forever?"

Beth's expression softened. "Best friends forever."

They were quiet for a while as the morning progressed around them. Mariel's gaze drifted to the window, and she wondered if the magic of the Zookeeper's world had somehow touched hers. Everything seemed different this morning. Maybe her summer wasn't going to turn out so bad, after all.

A chuckle from Beth interrupted her musings. "You know, it's hard to believe that so many people could be so…so *wrong*. It's a crazy world out there."

Mariel smiled wistfully. "Yes, it is," she agreed softly. "A real menagerie."

THE END

About the Author

Joanne Duncalf is a writer, entrepreneur, radiographer and former instructor of radiology. She belongs to the National Writers Association and the Christian Writers Fellowship International. Being a conservative advocate, she is also actively involved in American politics. She is a mother of three and a grandmother of six.